MARIE FERRARELLA

A Cavanaugh Christmas

ROMANTIC
SUSPENSE

Recycling programs
for this product may
not exist in your area.

ISBN-13: 978-0-373-27753-7

A CAVANAUGH CHRISTMAS

Books by Marie Ferrarella

MARIE FERRARELLA

This *USA TODAY* bestselling and RITA® Award-winning author has written more than two hundred books for Harlequin Books and Silhouette Books, some under the name Marie Nicole. Her romances are beloved by fans worldwide. Visit her website at www.marieferrarella.com.

To
Patience Bloom,
with undying gratitude
for allowing me
to be me

Chapter 1

"Boy, some guys sure get all the luck."

The comment, half complaint, half good-natured envy, came from thirty-five-year-old Detective Angelo LaGuardia and was directed at the man he'd called a partner for the past two and a half years, ever since the latter had been assigned to the Missing Persons Division of the Aurora Police Department. LaGuardia, married for sixteen years to the woman he'd met his first day in high school, viewed his partner's life much the way a man on a restricted diet viewed an ice-cream sundae—with strong, unfulfilled longing.

"First you go from being an annoying Italian," Angelo continued, getting more specific when his partner glanced up from his computer screen, puzzled, "to an annoying crown prince—"

Detective First Class Thomas Cavelli's sharp blue

eyes narrowed. "I'm not a crown prince." There was a steely emphasis just beneath his ordinarily easygoing, laid-back drawl, as well as a warning look in his eyes. "And, as far as I know, I've never been accused of being annoying."

His sister, Kendra, another recently relocated member of the Aurora Police Department, chose that moment to walk by the detectives' desks on her way out on a case. Younger than Tom by three years, Kendra chimed in her two cents' worth even as she kept on walking.

"That is definitely up for a vote, big brother."

"See?" Angelo declared with a measure of triumph, rocking back in his chair, a wide grin on his equally wide face.

"No one asked you, Kenny," Tom pointed out, raising his voice so that it followed his sister out. And then he turned back to his partner. LaGuardia was built as short and squat as he himself was tall and lean. "You said 'first.'"

Tom braced himself for what came next, knowing he'd hear it eventually. Might as well get it over with sooner than later.

LaGuardia's head bobbed up and down in affirmation. "That I did."

When no more words followed, Tom prompted him. "Which means there's a 'second.'"

LaGuardia laughed shortly as he nodded more to himself than to his partner. "Easy to see why you made detective—even without your blue-blood connections."

Though he didn't show it, the flippant term rankled Tom.

Unlike some of his brothers and sisters, when the

bombshell hit that the seven of them and their father were actually Cavanaughs rather than Cavellis, the way they had all grown up believing, Tom had more or less taken the news in stride. It was part of his basic philosophy of life: to deal with what was before him and then move on. So far, that philosophy had stood him in good stead.

It would be interesting to see if that would continue.

Tom reasoned that, Italian or Scottish, he was still the same person he'd been, still followed baseball games, particularly those of the Anaheim Angels, was still indifferent to the Lakers and the whole basketball scene in general. He still wrote with his left hand and operated power tools—when he actually had the time— with his right.

And he still intended to work his way up through the department on his own merits and not by riding on the coattails of his siblings or his father. That went double for the coattails of the family he and the others suddenly and completely without warning found themselves a part of.

It was barely two months ago that the news had surfaced, traveling through every nook and cranny in the Aurora Police Department with the speed of a lightning bolt. It was hard to say who in the family had been the most surprised. They all had been shell-shocked by the news for a little while. Some more so than others.

It all boiled down to this: because of a mix-up in the hospital, his father, Sean, a newborn, was accidentally switched with another newborn male of the same size and weight bearing the same first name and a very similar last name.

And that, in a nutshell, was how Sean Cavanaugh became Sean Cavelli and vice versa.

The Sean who had actually *been* a Cavelli, their father was informed, had died before he reached the age of one. He was a victim of SIDS, an innocuous collection of letters that stood for sudden infant death syndrome, the insidious, mysterious disease that claimed so many infant lives and had snuffed out the real Sean Cavelli's life.

Blissfully ignorant of all this, Tom's father had gone on to grow up the youngest in a family of two brothers and two sisters, married Theresa O'Brien, had seven children with her and had lived a good, full life. By an odd twist of fate, he'd gone on to join the forensic lab in a nearby city.

With that in the background, Tom had been rather surprised to hear—right after the bombshell hit—his father confess that he'd always felt as if he was standing outside the family circle. That, try as he might, he just didn't feel part of the family in the true, one hundred percent way that he longed to, despite the fact that everyone had always been nothing but kind to him.

Unable to pinpoint why, he'd always felt, for lack of a better word, "different." Once he found out that he was actually a Cavanaugh and not a Cavelli, he understood why. It all began to make sense to him.

Something within him had been calling out to the parents who had actually given him life. Calling out to the people through whose veins ran the same blood as his. Once the mystery was unraveled, Sean no longer felt like a duck out of water.

Still, to say that the news ushered in an emotional upheaval within his tight-knit family was putting it mildly. Be that as it may, Tom had prided himself on being able to roll with the punches, no matter which direction they came from.

But he *did* have trouble with, though he did his best to keep his reaction under wraps, being viewed differently by the people who worked alongside of him. Some of them just *assumed* he would change because of the very nature of his connection to the family that some viewed as police department royalty.

That really bothered him.

Tom knew that, for the most part, LaGuardia was kidding. But even so, he also suspected that there was just the tiniest kernel of truth in what the older man had just said. Angelo, as well as several others in the department, *did* perceive him to be a "crown prince" of sorts because not only was the chief of detectives a Cavanaugh—Brian—but the former chief of police—Andrew—was a Cavanaugh, as well.

And that didn't even *begin* to take into account the rest of the clan which was so prominently present on the police force. It was a standing joke that the Cavanaughs needed only a few more members in order to form their own country.

Now he was part of that, part of *them*—whether he chose to be or not.

Oh, there was no pressure—neither Brian nor Andrew were known for being the sort to apply undue pressure to get their own way. But pressure or not, that didn't change the reality of things. He'd thought of himself as a Cavelli from the first moment he realized that people had last names—and now he was a Cavanaugh, whether he acknowledged the fact by embracing the new last name or not.

Blood was blood.

A German shepherd was still a German shepherd even though his owner might proclaim him to be an Irish wolfhound. Like it or not, the Cavanaughs were perceived differently. And Tom didn't want to be treated differently. He'd worked too hard for that.

"So what's the second thing you're bemoaning?" Tom asked again since LaGuardia had deliberately left him hanging—and waiting impatiently. The man might be bursting with information, but he still liked to be coaxed to reveal it. Tom knew he'd have no peace until he obliged and played along with the game.

"And now *that* walks into your life," Angelo said, clearly envious as he gestured toward the tall, leggy redhead who had just crossed the threshold and entered the squad room.

It was all Tom could do to keep his mouth from dropping open. Looking at the woman was like seeing the sunrise for the very first time. Hard to put into words, but definitely affecting.

Tom silently reminded himself to breathe.

The woman moved with precision, as if each step had been measured out and allowed only so much distance to be used before the next step began.

Poetry embodied in a physical form, Tom caught himself thinking as he struggled to maintain a poker face.

Tom shifted his chair a little to get a better view. No doubt about it, the woman was exceedingly beautiful. She was also as serious looking as a judge rendering the date of a convicted killer's execution.

"From where I'm sitting," he observed, his voice deceptively mild, "she's walking into the squad room, not my life."

LaGuardia ignored the protest. "But she *is* heading for you."

Tom shifted his chair back to look at his partner, sitting at the desk next to his. "And you know this how?" he challenged.

Wide, sloping shoulders rose and fell in a careless fashion. "I keep my ear to the ground."

"That explains why you're so hunched over all the time," Tom quipped. But LaGuardia appeared to be adamant, so he asked, "Seriously, why would you think—"

"Overheard her talking to the old man," Angelo confessed, lowering his voice as if to keep this source between the two of them. "This one doesn't beat around the bush." There was admiration in his voice as he watched the woman make her way across the wide room littered with desks and personnel. "She went straight to the top to get her information."

Tom wondered exactly what information his partner was referring to. First things first, though. LaGuardia had a tendency to be vague at times. "She talked to Lt. Chambers?" he asked, referring to their direct superior in the division.

"Nope, to your new guardian angel—the chief of Ds himself," LaGuardia added when Tom focused his intense blue eyes on him, silently telling his partner to get to the point.

"And she asked for me?" There was a hint of mocking in Tom's question. He didn't know who the woman was and he sincerely doubted if she knew him, so there was no way she would be asking for him. This had to be LaGuardia's lame idea of a joke.

No doubt irritated by the mocking note in his partner's voice, LaGuardia said peevishly, "When she talked to your new uncle, she asked for the person with the best track record for finding missing children."

"Best" in this case was still not good enough in Tom's opinion. "Best" to him would have meant that he located the children every time one was reported missing or kidnapped instead of only seventy percent, which was where his record stood at the moment.

According to the law of averages, that was something to be proud of, his father had told him. But he had no patience—or the time—for pride. There'd be time enough for pride when every child's file that came across his desk was marked "closed" and it had been resolved with a happy ending.

And a happy ending occurred only when the child was found.

Alive.

Tom's doubts as to the veracity of LaGuardia's claim began to dissipate as the tall, willowy redhead drew closer. Apparently the woman *was* heading straight for his desk.

It crossed his mind that this could still be either La-Guardia's idea of a joke, or someone else's. Someone who wanted to pull his leg. If so, whoever was orchestrating this had to have a black sense of humor. There was nothing remotely amusing about the set of circumstances that would bring a woman to him, seeking his professional help. Had he not been as content and well adjusted as he was, Tom was fairly certain that his job, particularly the failures that went hand in hand with the caseload, would have haunted him beyond the point of human tolerance.

He wasn't sure how others survived within this particular environment, but as for him, for the most part, he focused on the successes. Focused on them to almost the exclusion of all else because he knew he had to keep a good, optimistic frame of mind in order to keep on doing what he was doing. And he had to keep going because there were children who needed someone to find them, to bring them home and to punish the person or persons who were responsible for having taken them away in the first place.

For a moment, his thought froze in place as he watched the woman coming closer, a lyrical song in heels that were far from sensible. It struck him that, despite her austere expression, this woman cared about appearances. At least her own.

She was a long way from home.

The thought came out of nowhere, in response to nothing in particular. But it was true. And it was for the first time.

In this day and age of facilitated travel, Detective Kaitlyn Two Feathers, of the Taos, New Mexico, Police Department, had never been outside of New Mexico, scarcely out of Taos, actually.

At least, not to her knowledge.

She'd been in her maternal grandmother's care the first four years of her life until the state, alerted by an anonymous "good citizen," had become aware of what was happening and had ultimately taken her away. Grandmothers weren't supposed to try to sell their unmarried daughter's child, even if that daughter was serving twenty to life for second-degree murder of said child's father.

It was quite possible that, in her grandmother's efforts to sell her—the woman and her boyfriend needed money to support their ever-growing dependence on drugs—she might have been taken across a state line or two. But since she had no extensive recollection of that time, it didn't count.

Wanderlust hadn't brought her to Aurora, a city in Northern California, but a promise. A promise she had given to a distraught mother who had begged her to bring back her baby. That the woman also happened to be her cousin just made the promise much more urgent and personal. It was a promise she had every intention of keeping, even if it wound up taking her to hell and back.

So far, though, it had only taken her to Aurora, California. She'd come as fast as she could, and with any luck she would still be in time to save Megan Willows before the four-year-old was completely swallowed up without a trace.

She'd promised to reunite mother and child by Christmas, and that meant within two weeks, leaving her with little time. She didn't plan on wasting any of it.

As she drew closer—close enough for Tom to become aware of a fresh, herbal scent—her brilliant blue eyes swept over the nameplates on both desks. The perusal brought a slight reproving frown of confusion on the woman's full lips.

"I'm looking for Detective Thomas Cavanaugh," she said in a voice that reminded a man of golden whiskey being poured into glass used only for very, very special occasions. "Do either of you know where I might be able to find him?"

The question was directed at both men as she studied each, one at a time.

"Right there," Angelo volunteered, pointing to his partner.

Tom noticed that LaGuardia pressed his lips together—probably to keep from literally drooling as he gaped at the woman.

For good measure, Kait looked down again at the nameplate on the man's desk. This time, there was displeasure in her frown. The nameplate didn't read Cavanaugh, it read Cavelli.

Kait didn't appreciate being jerked around. She'd had more than her share of that for a good part of her life. As first a police officer, then as the youngest officer to make detective, she'd had to prove herself over and over again. It got to be almost a daily event for the first year and a half, until the men she worked with began to take her seriously. Began to see that she intended to stay whether they approved of her or not.

Eventually, they had come around. Not all of them, but enough. Enough to make her life just the slightest bit easier if she chose to take that route.

For her part, Kait wanted no favors. She just wanted not to be harassed so that she could do her job the way she was meant to. Eventually, by the very nature of her dedication and her character, she won the respect she wanted.

But she took none of it for granted, knowing that each day would have challenges. Challenges she intended to meet and win.

"Your nameplate says Thomas Cavelli," she pointed out, nodding at it.

"Yeah, it does," Tom acknowledged.

His eyes drifted over the length of her. She was lean, but no pushover. He'd bet a large sum of money that beneath that fitted gray jacket and straight skirt was a muscular body. She didn't do it to look good, he decided. She did it to be fit. To be ready.

But ready for what?

And what was a woman who looked like that doing here? She certainly wasn't someone who'd recently had a child go missing. She bore none of the telltale signs of a woman who'd been suddenly stamped with tragedy. Nor did she appear distraught and holding it together for the sake of the child who had been lost or abducted.

She smelled of something fresh and herbal, not of rampant fear.

So who was she and why had the chief of detectives sent her here—if he actually had?

Tom cast a skeptical side glance at his partner. But LaGuardia struggled not to visibly salivate as he hung on every syllable that passed over the woman's perfectly shaped lips. If Angelo had put the mystery woman up to this, he would have taken more of a backseat to what was being played out before him.

"So which is it?" Kait asked. A hint of impatience wove through her voice. "Cavanaugh or Cavelli?"

It occurred to her that no matter which name it wound up being, someone as handsome as this man was undoubtedly far too consumed with his own appearance to be very good at anything else. He was probably someone's son and had risen through the ranks because of that rather than any actual merit.

"That is the question," Tom responded, the corners of his mouth curving ever so slightly.

And that, indeed, was the question. The question each of them had to tackle on their own. He and his siblings each had to make up their minds how to handle this new earthquake in their lives. Did they continue life beneath the moniker they'd always responded to? Did they stay Cavellis? Or did they switch over to the new name which, according to sworn testimony from the hospital administrator, was the right one?

Cavelli or Cavanaugh, which would it be?

Obviously, the chief of detectives had already made up his own mind about the matter.

"That's a boring story for a rainy afternoon over a bracing glass of bourbon," Tom told her easily, his eyes never leaving her face. "The more important one is what brought you here?"

He got down to business quickly, Kait thought. She could appreciate that.

Taking a small, almost imperceptible bracing breath, Kait dug into her jacket pocket and took out her wallet. It contained exactly one credit card, her license, a few bills totaling eight dollars—and her official police identification.

She flipped her wallet open and held up her ID for the quiet, scrutinizing detective to see. "I'm Detective Kaitlyn Two Feathers—"

She got no further than that.

"Two Feathers?" LaGuardia echoed. He stared at the torrent of red hair which seemed in direct contradiction to the Native American surname on her identification.

"Yes," she replied. There was just the slightest hint of humor in her eyes. The detective wasn't the first person to react this way upon first hearing her last name. "Two Feathers."

Tom took a less brash approach. "Husband?" he asked mildly, since the woman before him looked no more Native American than he did.

Actually, he probably could pass for Native American more easily since he had the dark, almost blue-black hair that was so prevalent among the people of the tribes sprinkled throughout the United States.

"Why?" Kait countered. Her eyes met his in a steady, unwavering gaze. "Do I need one?"

"Not in my book," LaGuardia piped up before Tom could answer. One look at the older man and Tom could see that his partner was badly smitten with this commanding, unsmiling woman.

"You don't need anything," Tom informed her mildly. "It's just that you don't look like a Native American, so I thought maybe that was your married name."

He glanced down at her left hand. She wore only a watch. A man's watch by the look of it, since it seemed too large for her. A gift? Something to remember someone by? In either case, that was the only form of adornment the redhead had on either hand. Beyond that, there were no rings, official or otherwise. No bracelets and no piercings of any sort.

He got the distinct impression that she was hiding something, something that went beyond her unusual surname. He couldn't help thinking this was a woman of secrets.

He grew more intrigued by the moment.

Chapter 2

The handsome detective's reaction wasn't anything new. Kait was used to people looking at her with a puzzled expression the first time they learned her last name.

She could almost read their thoughts: *but you don't look like a Native American.*

There was a reason for that. More specifically, there was a reason why she didn't look like a Navajo, which in her case was the tribe the name had originated from. She didn't look like a Navajo because she wasn't one.

As close as Kait could figure, she was part Irish, part Welsh and part mutt most likely. The mother she couldn't remember and the grandmother she wished she didn't hadn't exactly had the time or the inclination to talk to her, much less ruminate about her roots and her heritage.

Her mother had been forced to give her up when Kait was only a few days old—something she assumed the woman who gave birth to her did gladly since Kait's very existence was a reminder of the man her mother had been convicted of killing in a jealous rage.

Her mother had given her to her own mother. Her grandmother, Ada, had kept her around not out of any sort of love, but because she turned out to be useful. Ada quickly discovered, much to her happiness, that people were more apt to be lenient and forgiving of a woman caught stealing if the theft had been committed in an attempt to feed her granddaughter.

At least that was what her grandmother told anyone who would listen whenever she *was* caught.

That sort of thing went on for a couple of years— until Kait grew out of her "cute baby" stage. When that happened, her grandmother had tried to earn a profit in a more cut-and-dried sort of way—by selling her outright.

Or trying to.

Convinced that a childless couple would pay top dollar for a "little one of their own," her grandmother had approached one such unsavory candidate, asking for "a rock-bottom price."

The man turned out to possess a remnant of a conscience, and he called the police to tip them off about what Ada was trying to do. The police in turn set up a sting, sending in two officers to pose as a couple desperate to start a family at all costs. The sting went down and her grandmother was sent to prison. Ironically, the same one where her mother was serving time and where she herself had started life.

The name of the police officer who had been part of

the sting was Ronald Two Feathers. It was his name that she proudly bore and had for a number of years now.

But Kaitlyn saw no reason to explain any of that, or to tell the two detectives sitting at their desks—even the kneecap-melting, good-looking one—how the name eventually became hers legally. Nor did she intend to tell them that the missing little girl belonged to Ronald's niece. Family matters were private to her. Besides, knowing her background made no difference one way or the other, and as far as they were concerned, it didn't affect why she was here.

As a matter of fact, had she lived the perfect American life—instead of the exact opposite for the first twelve of those years—she still would have been here, searching for Megan. Been here because of the desperate look in her cousin Amanda Willows's eyes as she begged her to find her little girl, her baby.

Amanda's husband—and Megan's father—was deployed overseas. It had taken two days to reach Corporal Derek Willows through channels, and now the young Marine was flying home to be with his wife in their time of anguish. Because of the zigzag pattern of the connecting flights, he would be here just before Christmas. More than anything in the world, Kait wanted to give the young couple something to celebrate, not mourn. It was the least she could do, if for no other reason than she owed it to Ronald.

Unzipping the heavily creased leather binder she was carrying, Kait took out an enlarged, eight-by-ten photograph of a little girl with curly, dark brown hair. The photo had been taken at an amusement park on Megan's last birthday. She was looking directly into the camera, and it was the smile and the bright eyes that immediately captured the viewer's attention. The smile was so wide, so radiant and so genuine, it seemed almost three-dimensional as it jumped off the page.

"This is Megan Willows," Kait said in a voice that seemed stripped of all emotion. "Nearly four days ago, she was abducted right out of her own front yard by a man driving a white van."

Tom raised his eyes from the photograph to look at the woman who had brought this to him.

Four days.

In almost ninety percent of the cases, four days was practically a death sentence. The expression in the woman's eyes told him she was aware of that. It was obvious that she chose not to focus on the grim prognosis but on the successful recovery of the child.

At first glance, optimism would have been the last thing he would have associated with the red-haired detective.

"Where's the little girl's home?" Tom asked.

"Taos. New Mexico," Kait added after a beat. She was quick to cut him off before he could say the obvious. "And yes, I know I have no authority here, which is why I spoke to your chief of detectives first. He said it was all right if I worked the case, as long as you were there to supervise."

There was more, a lot more, but he didn't need to know that. Didn't need to know that she wasn't here in *any* sort of official capacity. Didn't need to know that once her personal connection to the kidnapped girl had come to light, she'd been taken off the case no matter how much she'd asked not to be. His knowing wouldn't help her find the little girl.

She paused a moment before continuing. "I usually

work alone, but I'd be willing to work with the devil himself if it meant getting Megan back safe and sound."

"The devil's not available," Tom commented. "I guess you'll have to make do with me for the time being." He glanced down at the photograph again. If that was his daughter and she went missing, he would be willing to move heaven and earth to find her. Was that what the detective with the deep blue eyes was doing? Moving everything in sight as she looked for a trail? "If this happened in New Mexico, what are you doing here?"

"One very sharp little boy playing across the street copied down the van plates while his sister ran into the house to get Megan's mother—apparently it was a play-date and Mrs. Willows was supposed to be watching the children." Kait's mouth twisted slightly in a smile she didn't feel. "Unfortunately, she'd just stepped inside to get the kids some snacks. The abductor saw his chance, swooped in and grabbed the little girl before anyone knew what was happening. *Her* little girl." As Kait related the story, she could actually feel Amanda's pain. "It's obvious that whoever took the child planned this abduction very carefully. My guess is that he had been watching her, learning if there was a route."

She used her words judiciously, Tom noted. He watched the detective's face as he asked, "Abduction, not kidnapping?"

Kait shook her head. "No. There's been no ransom call or note. No demands made and no contact of any kind. This was someone who targeted Megan specifically, for a reason."

Even as she said the words, they tasted like bitter herbs in her mouth. This kind of an abduction meant the person who had abducted the little girl was either a pedophile or he had taken Megan, who was exceedingly pretty, in order to sell her.

It was the latter possibility that had raised a red flag in Kaitlyn's mind. Someone might be trying to sell the child the way her grandmother had tried to sell her. That kind of thing wasn't supposed to happen in a country like this. Not ever.

And yet it did. More times than she would even allow herself to think about.

The detective from New Mexico had said two things that had caught Tom's attention and raised questions in his mind. She'd mentioned that *she* had talked to Brian, not that her superior had placed a call to the chief of detectives and spoken with him. Was that just a slip of her tongue, or was she off the reservation, so to speak, and acting on her own?

The spontaneous phrase evoked a hint of a smile to his lips. Under the circumstances, given the woman's last name, he knew that she would most likely deem the harmless cliché inappropriate. He was relieved that he'd thought it rather than asked it, though he'd meant no disrespect. But Detective Two Feathers didn't appear to him to have a sense of humor.

She saw his smile before he managed to suppress it. "Something about this case strike you as funny, Detective?"

"No, not at all," he replied soberly. And that brought him to his second question, which he'd asked already. "So, you didn't answer me. What brought you here?"

"The van had out-of-state license plates," she told him. "When I ran them, it turns out that the vehicle was a rental and it belongs to a California rental agency. Specifically, a rental agency located right here in Aurora." She would have gone to the FBI with this, but there was no proof that the van ever returned to California. She needed more evidence before the bureau could be called in.

At least there was some kind of trail, Tom thought. The next question that occurred to him was one he regarded as rhetorical. "Have you gone to see them yet?"

He didn't get the answer he expected.

Kaitlyn had wanted to, but her hands were tied by protocol. There were times—such as this—that she wished she'd become a private investigator instead of following in Ronald Two Feathers' footsteps. P.I.s had more leeway and freedom in the way they operated. Red tape and tedious procedures drove her crazy, forcing her to walk when she wanted to run or fly.

"No, I have not," she told him, far from pleased with the admission. "That's what I need you for."

The word *need* seemed to almost shimmer before him for a split second before he banked it down and forced himself to focus on the situation.

Even so, he could literally *feel* LaGuardia looking on enviously. He was surprised that his partner was keeping as quiet as he was. Ordinarily, he jumped right into the conversation, eager to be a part of whatever was going down.

"Always nice to be needed," Tom commented. The remark was meant to be light, not a come-on, but he could sense the woman's back going up. They would need to have a few things cleared up at the outset. "You know, you might want to lighten up a little. I think we'll get along much better if you do."

"I have no interest in 'getting along,' Detective," she

informed him, forcing herself to sound distant and cool. "I just want to find the missing girl. Now can you help me, or do I go back to your chief of detectives and tell him he has to assign someone else to the case?"

She was challenging him. But this wasn't going to work if she wanted him to jump through hoops. That wasn't the way he worked.

"That depends."

Her eyes narrowed, as did her mouth. "On what, exactly?" she asked.

Tom minced no words. She didn't strike him as the type who valued subtlety, but would rather get to the point.

"On whether you intend to carry around that chip on your shoulder the entire time you're here, because I can tell you right now, that chip isn't going to fit into my car."

Out of the corner of his eye, he saw LaGuardia looking at him in utter surprise. Ordinarily, if he was any more easygoing, he'd be accused of being asleep. But easygoing didn't mean pushover, and he had no intentions of being run over by this woman, no matter how sexy she appeared to be.

"I don't have a chip on my shoulder," Kait informed him. He continued looking at her, as if silently saying that they both knew better than that.

Kait frowned. Coming here was a bad idea, but what else could she do? She needed both the authority and the file access that being connected with the local police department afforded. She'd left on her own, telling Lt. Blackwell that she was taking a vacation—the first that anyone had known her to take.

The lieutenant had looked at her with suspicion in

his eyes, but said nothing about the case or her direct involvement in it. He'd merely nodded.

And then, on a parting note, he'd said almost under his breath, "You have to do what you have to do."

It told her that even though he didn't want to be officially "informed," Lieutenant Philip Blackwell knew what she was up to. Knew that she was determined to act on her own despite the fact that their police department was far too understaffed to have any of its detectives go running off to parts unknown in hopes of bringing down a predator and returning a child into her parents' arms. And she could see that the lieutenant privately wished her well. And that he could be counted on to keep her spot open for her until she returned. By Christmas. The way she'd promised.

"All right," she said purely for Cavanaugh-Cavelli's benefit and not because she intended to behave any differently than she normally did. "I'll see about parking my so-called 'chip' somewhere for the duration." Her gaze all but heated his chair to the boiling point. "*Now* will you come with me?" she asked.

Tom was already on his feet. He slipped his somewhat rumpled jacket on over his holstered, department-issued firearm.

"To the ends of the earth," he quipped.

Terrific. Just what she needed as a temporary partner. A comedian.

"Just to the car-rental agency will suffice. It's located on Third and Grand," she added since he needed to know where he was heading. She started walking toward the doorway.

"Hold it," he called after her. "I've got to tell Lt. Chambers that I'm going to be—"

"It's already been taken care of," she assured him, then because he looked at her skeptically, she added, "I was there when your uncle called Lt. Chambers in order to—"

Just the slightest trace of irritation broke through the carefully varnished veneer as Tom tersely informed the woman, "He's not my uncle."

She was certain she'd gotten the family connection right. Since she'd been denied family for most of her life, she had a kind of built-in radar when it came to things like that. Why would the chief of detectives refer to the detective as his nephew if it wasn't so?

"Family feud?" she guessed. The tone of her voice sounded so detached that it seemed to indicate she couldn't really care less if he was feuding with the chief of Ds or not, as long as it didn't get in the way of her finding the little girl.

The term *family* feud was far too leading as far as Tom was concerned. He knew Brian Cavanaugh from two brief meetings. Both times he'd been part of a group. He'd accompanied his father and his siblings when they had gone over to the former chief of police's rambling and surprisingly welcoming house.

During those two times he'd exchanged perhaps half a dozen words with Brian Cavanaugh, perhaps less.

But of course he knew the man by reputation. Everyone did. Brian Cavanaugh was a fair man and a good leader, never asking anyone to do anything that he wouldn't do himself. Those closest to him—not just his family but also the officers who served under him— would gladly follow him to hell and back if he asked.

Outside of a handful of criminals, the man had no known enemies. Everyone respected and liked the chief of detectives. And even though Tom wasn't as reluctant to be assimilated by the Cavanaugh clan as some of his brothers and sisters were, he still wanted to do it at his own pace, on his own terms. As Popeye had so eloquently put it, he'd quipped to his father after the first en masse meeting, "I am what I am and that's all that I am." And changing his surname from one thing to another made no difference to the man he was deep down at the core.

In like fashion, he always had and still did like to have a vote when it came to things that affected his life, be it privately or in the field. And, in this case, what it boiled down to was that he didn't like not being consulted before being thrust headlong into this investigation.

In essence he was being shipped off to wet-nurse this woman-with-a-mission, and no one had asked him whether or not he had any objections to his new assignment.

Now who's acting as if he has a chip on his shoulder? a small voice in his head wanted to know. He was irritated with himself and with the fact that he'd allowed his reaction to show enough so that even this stranger had taken notice.

"No," he replied quietly. "Just going through a period of adjustment, that's all."

She glanced at him, puzzled. "You lost me."

No such luck, Tom thought, the thin smile on his lips never wavering. She might not be a Native American by blood, but she looked as if she knew how to track a man through a snowstorm. Something about her demeanor told him she had the tenacity of a bulldog when it came to following a trail.

He supposed she'd already proved that, since she'd tracked down the kidnapper's van to the point of origin. All they needed right now were some answers, and as long as she was right about the van, they might just be lucky enough to get those answers. Quickly.

"Long story." He tossed off the words carelessly, hoping she'd take the hint and drop the subject.

She slanted a look in his direction. He couldn't tell if that was amusement or impatience on her face. Probably the latter. "Part of the one you're saving for a rainy day?"

He nodded. "One and the same."

There were windows running along the length of the back wall. She looked in their direction just before they left the squad room. "How often does it rain here?"

"Not often," he answered. "Although, when it does, it usually rains in the winter—and then it pours." They had an official rainy season—when it rained at all, which hadn't been often these past few years.

"Weatherman forecasts sun for the next week," she told him. Kaitlyn had checked that online just before coming here. She had wanted to be as prepared as she could for any and all possibilities.

"That's what we pay him to do," Tom quipped, tongue in cheek.

Just as he began to cross the threshold out into the hallway, Tom found he had to back up a little instead. Brian Cavanaugh had just gotten off the elevator and was on his way into the squad room at the same time.

Since two objects couldn't occupy the same space and still coexist peacefully with the laws of physics, Tom stepped aside so that his chief of detectives had dibs on the space.

The man nodded first at the willowy, attractive visitor who had just been in his office less than twenty minutes ago, then at his newly discovered nephew. His smile was easy, genuine. "I see Detective Two Feathers found you."

Tom forced a smile—or what passed as one—to his lips. "That she did."

And then the chief of detectives did something that Tom hadn't been expecting. He apologized. In a manner of speaking.

"I know I didn't ask you for your input on this— or how you felt about being teamed up with someone else, but from what I've been hearing from Chambers, you're the right man to lend the detective a hand." He paused, swiftly scrutinizing the younger man. "Unless you're working on something and would rather not walk away from it right now. If that's the case, I could assign someone else to help out Detective Two Feathers."

This left Tom with nothing to feel slighted about. Since the chief of Ds was consulting him about how he felt about being lent out, there was no reason for him to feel as if he had no say. And no reason, really, for him to turn the chief down.

Especially since he and LaGuardia had just closed a case two days ago—complete with a happy ending— and for a change no new case had come across their desks. And no one had asked either of them to work any of the cold cases that involved missing persons.

The only leg he might have had to stand on in order to beg off was if he had a genuine phobia about being forced to work with a new person. One of the other detectives in the squad room went through a chemical reaction each time one of his partners left, but Tom had no such difficulty adjusting. He liked different things. He felt they kept him fresh and on his toes.

And he had a hunch that the same description could be applied to working with Detective Kaitlyn Two Feathers. Besides, he found that he had a very deep desire to find out just exactly what made the sexy redhead tick.

"That won't be necessary, Chief." He glanced in her direction. "I'm looking forward to helping Detective Two Feathers any way I can."

Brian smiled, nodding. "Knew I could count on you, Tom." He looked to both of them. "Well, I'll get out of your way, then. And keep me posted," he called after them.

"Will do," Tom promised just before he stepped into the elevator behind the detective from New Mexico.

Chapter 3

For a moment back there, when they'd encountered the chief of detectives, Kaitlyn could feel her heart lodging itself in her throat. She was waiting to hear what the tall, genial-looking man *wasn't* saying. That he had gotten in contact with Lt. Blackwell about the case and had discovered that she was working this on her own. That she had come here unofficially, without any authority and completely without her superior's blessings, which meant that the chief of detectives was under no obligation to provide her with aid of any kind.

As a matter of fact, that would put him within his rights just to send her back to Taos with a warning never to come back.

When no mention had been made of any of this, Kait breathed a sigh of relief inwardly and felt—almost literally—that she had just dodged a bullet. At least as far as her career on the police force went. Privately, it wouldn't have changed a thing. She wouldn't have given up and docilely returned to New Mexico; it would have just become more difficult for her to proceed.

Difficult, but not impossible.

The way Kait saw it, she had already beaten the odds. By all rights, thanks to her grandmother, she really should have been dead a long time ago. Which meant that, as far as she was concerned, she was living on borrowed time and anything she accomplished on this "borrowed" time was simply her way of paying back whoever was watching over her.

She liked to think that the one watching over her these days was Ronald Two Feathers.

It only made sense. After all, he'd been nothing short of her guardian angel while he was alive, so why not really take over the role after he'd died?

The elevator came to a stop on the first floor and she and the detective got out. She found that in order to keep up with Tom and his incredibly long stride, she had to lengthen and quicken her own just short of skipping along. She wasn't a small woman, but neither was she six foot two the way he apparently was.

It wasn't until they'd gone down the ten steps from the front of the building to the parking lot situated in the back of the precinct that he turned toward her and said anything.

"Mine or yours?" he asked.

Caught off guard, she stared at him, trying to make sense of the question. "Excuse me?"

"Do you want to use my car or your car?"

Ordinarily, he would have just walked up to his own vehicle, an unmarked white Crown Victoria. But he had the feeling that when it came to this woman, presuming anything would irritate her.

To be truthful, Kait hadn't given something as trivial as mode of transportation any thought. Her mind was filled with the larger details, such as finding out the identity of the man or men who had abducted Megan Willows.

Since he asked, she gave him the first answer that came into her head. "What's wrong with my driving mine and you driving yours?"

"Well, for one thing, it's wasteful," he replied. "Overkill," he elaborated, then added, "I know the city, so it only makes sense that I drive."

Her eyes narrowed. He found himself intrigued rather than annoyed.

Did he think she was directionally challenged? Or that she couldn't read a map? She obviously could. She'd looked up the agency's exact location as soon as she obtained the actual address during her initial search. And she'd obviously driven her car from Taos to Aurora. She hadn't just stumbled onto the city through a stroke of dumb luck.

He didn't look like a Neanderthal, but looks could be deceiving. She had encountered enough men who dragged their knuckles and thought of her as being completely incapable and unsuitable for a law-enforcement career. She needed to set him straight right from the get-go.

"I didn't exactly wander into Aurora by accident. I do know how to find my way around."

There was just the slightest hint of humor in his eyes, even though he kept the smile from his lips as he nodded. "You're a natural-born pathfinder. Okay, you drive," he told her with no qualms. "I haven't got a problem with that."

Privacy was a very large component in her life these days. She didn't particularly like having to share a vehicle. At the very least, driving this man anywhere meant being responsible for driving the detective back to the precinct, and she preferred to be free to go wherever she needed to—whenever she wanted to. "I'd rather we went separately."

He eyed her for a moment, dissecting her words to get at her thought process. Rather than agree to drive separately, he took a guess at her motivation for isolation. "You have trust issues, don't you?"

The observation rankled her. Especially since it had come out of nowhere and was uncomfortably close to the truth. She nailed him with a pointed glare.

Rather than deny his assumption, she went on the attack. "I have 'issues' with people who try to analyze me."

He raised his hands to chest level, fingers pointed toward the sky as if in surrender. "Not trying to analyze you," he told her. "I'm just trying to find a way to get along with you."

She blew out an annoyed breath. "You have a very strange way of showing it."

Kait felt herself growing edgier. They didn't really have the time to stand around out here like this and argue like two dogs trying to mark their territory. Every wasted moment was a moment less she had to find Megan. Alive.

"All right, we'll go in your car," Kait bit off, then urged, "just let's go."

"Whatever you say," Tom responded, then gestured for her to follow him. "It's right over here."

Whatever you say. His phrase echoed in her head. *Yeah, right. As long as I say what you want,* she thought, struggling to keep her annoyance under wraps. She couldn't show him how much he irritated her. She needed this man. At least for now.

"How long have you been in missing persons?" Tom asked the transplanted New Mexican detective once they had pulled out of the parking lot and were on their way to the car-rental agency.

"I'm not," she answered stiffly, correcting his initial assumption. When he looked at her curiously, she explained, "We don't have divisions in the department the way you do out here. The police department back home is too small for that. Everyone on the force handles whatever comes our way—or at least we try to," she added almost under her breath.

Cutbacks had hit not just the big cities, but hers, as well. They were making do with a reduced police department, which was why no one had replaced her when she'd been taken off the case. That left only Juarez to carry on what there was of the investigation. Never mind that the man couldn't investigate his way out of a paper bag and he was trying to work the case from his desk rather than from the road.

"Can this thing go any faster?" she asked Tom impatiently. She had her doubts about the accuracy of the speedometer. It was registering sixty-five but it felt to her as if they were crawling.

"It can," he allowed. "But that would be really going

over the speed limit." He spared her a glance. "Wouldn't want me breaking any laws now, would you?"

She was accustomed to the men on the force back home bending the rules whenever they needed to, sometimes just because they wanted to. She was surprised that this detective didn't. Especially since he was related to the chief of detectives and had a get-out-of-jail-free card.

"Where I come from," she told him, "we do what we have to do."

"We pretty much do that here," Tom agreed. "We just don't abuse it."

"Meaning you think I would?" she challenged, taking offense.

"Just stating a fact, Detective. Don't look now," he said, lowering his voice, "but I think that chip of yours just hitched a ride in the back of my car."

She bit her lower lip to keep from retorting. Instead, she stared straight ahead at the road. It occurred to her that she'd mentioned the car rental agency's location only once during her initial conversation with the man and his partner. More than likely, he hadn't been paying close attention.

In her experience, men took it as an affront to their manhood to be put in a position where they had to ask for directions, but she had no intentions of having him drive around aimlessly.

So she asked him bluntly, "You do know where you're going, right?"

Tom smiled at her question. He was blessed with a memory that retained everything—from the important to the ridiculous—but for now he saw no need to tell her that. Given what he'd glimpsed of her disposition, she'd most likely think he was bragging.

"I always know where I'm going," he told her easily.

"How very lucky for you," she murmured under her breath.

It was a struggle, but Tom managed to keep his smile to himself.

Drive! Car Rental was an independent agency that depended on word-of-mouth, repeat business and extremely low rental fees to gain new clientele and to meet the monthly mortgage payments.

The agency certainly didn't rely on any sort of inviting charm—or even basic cleanliness, Kait thought as they pulled up into the long, narrow parking lot that was behind the small, rundown building. The rental agency was located at the end of a long block that had once housed a thriving strip mall and now had only, except for the rental agency, a collection of empty, single-story buildings to whisper of past glory days and successful businesses that had moved on, or ones that had gone under.

Tom automatically locked his car before they went in.

"Hello," the lanky clerk behind the counter said cheerfully. Slightly unkempt, with a stubborn, greasy stain in the middle of his lime-colored, wrinkled golf shirt, he sported a two-day growth he obviously thought made him look rugged, but in reality just added to the impression that hygiene was low on the list of his priorities.

He quickly stuck the magazine he'd been perusing beneath the counter so that it was out of sight. "Looking for some wheels to get around our fair city?" he asked brightly.

"Looking to see if you remember renting this vehicle to someone." Kait placed the information she'd secured in front of the man, turning the piece of paper around so that he could read it.

The sunny disposition immediately vanished. "Why?" the clerk asked, his eyes moving like loose black marbles from one face to the other. "You cops?"

"Right on the first guess," Tom mockingly marveled as he looked at the woman beside him. "You're a bright young man." Knowing what was coming next—a request for proof—Tom took out his wallet and held up his ID for the man's inspection. "Now, why don't you be a good citizen—Clark—" he said, reading the nameplate on the counter, "and go on that computer and see what kind of information you can come up with for us?"

"Would if I could," Clark answered petulantly. "But the computer's down. Been down for the last two days," he complained. "I think it's dead. That's why I'm reading a magazine," he moaned, as if reading something that used actual pages was a prehistoric endeavor that he found distasteful and beneath him.

"Mind if I take a look at it?" Tom asked.

Not waiting for a reply, Tom came around to the back of the counter and faced the dormant computer. It looked like a holdover from the last decade, a relic by most standards. The desktop was coupled with a clumsy old-fashioned preflat-screen monitor.

Business obviously had to be pretty bad lately, he judged.

"When was the last time you had this upgraded?"

he asked the clerk, feeling around the casing for an on button.

Faded, tuftlike eyebrows came together in a squiggly, confused line. "Huh?" Clark asked.

Well, that answered that, Tom thought. "Never mind."

It was very clear that the clerk knew nothing about the machine he'd most likely used to access porn more than anything else.

Tom turned the machine off and then on again, attempting to reboot the computer by going into the operating system's safe mode. As he worked, he secretly marveled at what a small world it really was. He was utilizing things he'd learned at an after-hours class that had been given at the precinct. The class had been led by one of his newfound cousins' wives—Brenda Cavanaugh. He'd taken the class before he'd ever been made aware of his connection to the family.

While he tried to get the computer up and running again, for the time being Tom left questioning the hapless clerk to Kaitlyn. He had a gut feeling that she was good at interrogations.

Kait began with the most basic of questions. "Do you have any surveillance cameras on the premises?"

"Got one out back." Clark jerked his thumb toward the rear, indicating the parking lot that was just beyond the back wall. "Boss put it in after two of the cars in the lot got stolen." Leaning in closer to her, the clerk lowered his voice and confided, "This ain't the safest neighborhood, you know." He said it as if he thought she wouldn't have guessed as much from the neighborhood's seedy appearance. And then he looked at her pointedly, as if she had it within her power to change things if she wanted to. "We could stand to have a few more cops around here."

"Couldn't we all?" Kait acknowledged, then nodded at the camera that was mounted by the door. Its lens was pointed directly at the counter. Why hadn't the clerk mentioned this one? "Where's the feed from that camera?"

The request confused Clark. He blinked. "The what again?"

"The feed," she repeated. "The old tapes or DVDs recorded by that camera. Where do you keep them?"

"We don't," the clerk answered very simply.

"Why not?" she demanded, then came up with a possible answer. "You reuse them?"

If they were recorded over, the situation could still be salvaged. The computer tech at the police station might be able to undo the layers, separate them so that the recordings beneath could be viewed. At least it was something to hope for, better than nothing.

Clark shook his head, strands of his hair, which was on the long side, moving about his thin face independently.

"No, I mean that's just a dummy. The camera's just for show," he said, seeming so proud when he elaborated. "People think twice before jumping you if they think it's all gonna be caught on video."

So much for catching their perpetrator in the act of renting the vehicle. That meant the case was now riding on the surveillance recordings from the camera trained on the parking lot in the back.

Struggling to harness her impatience, Kait glanced over toward Tom and the computer he was working on. The expression on his face didn't give her much hope.

"How's that coming?" she asked, raising her voice in order to catch his attention.

His fingers stopped moving across the keyboard. With a resigned sigh, Tom frowned. "I'm afraid this isn't going to be much help."

So near and yet so far. Damn it, anyway. "It's dead?" she asked him, not bothering to hide her frustration at this point.

"Oh, no," he contradicted. "I got it to run and even pulled up the transaction involving our friend and the white van."

That was exactly what she was hoping for. Yet Cavelli didn't look like a man who'd just witnessed a breakthrough. She braced herself to receive the disappointing news.

"Then what's the problem?" she asked.

"Well, if the address on the guy's license is correct, then the guy we're after lives in the middle of the bay. I mean *really* in the bay. Your missing little girl was abducted by Aquaman."

"That's a lie," Clark piped up. "Aquaman would never do that. I've got every one of his comics in my collection and he's just too honorable," the clerk insisted indignantly. "Besides, I don't remember him coming in."

"I guess Mensa won't be asking him to join their club anytime soon," Tom quipped. And then he realized that maybe he was talking over the other detective's head. He'd been guilty of that before, as his partner was always quick to point out to him. "That's a club where the IQ has to be—"

Kait cut him off. "I *know* what Mensa is," she informed him coldly.

Tom laughed softly. The sound rippled along her skin. She attributed it to her lack of a decent night's sleep ever since she'd left New Mexico.

"That puts you one up on LaGuardia," Tom told her. "He's always complaining that half the time he doesn't know what I'm talking about."

She moved to the other side of the counter to see exactly what it was that the Aurora detective had pulled up on the screen. She found herself looking at a blurry photograph of a rather portly man who appeared as if he could run through a brick wall and shake the effects off.

"The photo," she said to the clerk, calling his attention to the screen. "Is that the face of the man you remember renting this van?" Kait tapped the paper with the vehicle information on it for good measure.

Clark squinted at the screen. "I remember him from somewhere," he admitted slowly. "Coulda been the guy who rented the van."

At this point, she was going to have to go with that. "Good enough," Kait declared. "We'll print it."

Tom was ready to oblige. There was only one problem. He looked around, but didn't see what he needed.

"Great," he said to Kait. "Now all we need is a printer."

Clark instantly brightened up, like a puppy eager to do a trick and be rewarded for it with a treat. With a little bit of fanfare, the clerk reached under the counter, right next to his magazine.

"Got it right here," he announced. Taking the printer in both hands, Clark relocated it to the far edge of the counter.

Kait looked at it, then at the clerk. Her expression was incredulous.

"You're kidding, right?" The printer Clark had produced was an early-model dot matrix.

Crestfallen, he protested, "Hey, we don't throw money away on luxuries. This works. Sometimes," Clark added as an afterthought and in a much lower, almost inaudible voice.

Beggars couldn't be choosers, she told herself. "All right, print it up—and send a copy to this email address," she added suddenly.

The instruction was to Tom rather than the clerk. She suspected that was the only way she would be able to get a colored version of the license photograph, via email that she would print herself. As for the black-and-white copy that the dot matrix struggled with, that might just give them something to use with the facial-recognition program. With luck, they might be able to match the man to something or someone that *wasn't* located out in the middle of the ocean.

"You keep all the rental cars out back?" she asked.

Clark bobbed his head up and down again. "We sure do."

She was taking nothing for granted. "And that camera you have mounted in the back lot, it works?"

The clerk was beaming as he gestured toward the small screen that was feeding them back the picture from the parking lot. "Look for yourself."

Seeing something on the screen wouldn't do her any good if the recordings hadn't been kept. "Do you keep the recordings?" she asked again.

This time Clark appeared a little sheepish. "I've been meaning to erase them so we can use 'im again. Quality ain't too good after ten or twelve times, but like I said—"

She suppressed a sigh. "You don't have money for luxuries, yes, I know. I—we," she corrected herself as she felt Tom glancing her way, "need the recording from the date the van was rented."

"Okay," Clark replied in such a vague way, Kait had the impression that she was losing him.

"Has it been brought back?" she asked, enunciating each word as if trying to communicate with someone who was more than a little mentally challenged.

"Not yet. But he paid for two weeks up front, so I don't figure it'll be back before then."

So much for going over the van with all the technology the CSI had available. "Of course not."

A movement on the screen caught her attention as she took the black-and-white photograph that Tom had finally finished printing for her. When she got a better view of the surveillance monitor and saw what was happening, she was startled.

The next second, she turned on the heel of her boot and raced out of the office and straight to the parking lot.

Chapter 4

Gut instincts had Tom taking off after the woman.

"Why are we running?" he called after her.

It surprised him that she could run faster than he'd given her credit for. Tom found he had to step up his own pace to catch up—which he did just before she rounded the side of the rental building. She was obviously heading for the parking lot in the back.

"There are three thugs trying to steal your car," Kait tossed over her shoulder.

"Good reason."

Tom had pulled out his service weapon and had it at the ready before she could even finish answering his question.

What happened next, when Kait reviewed it in her mind later, had all taken place incredibly fast and yet, somehow, it felt as if it was unfolding in slow motion, as well.

At least it did to her.

One second she and the Aurora detective had just reached the back of the squat building where the parking lot full of secondhand vehicles stood waiting to be rented out for the right price. The next she heard Cavelli or whatever his name was loudly proclaiming a single word, "Gun!"

Just like that, before she could hone in on where the weapon was and which of the thugs was pointing it, Kait felt herself being pushed down to the ground. Not just pushed down to the ground, but, at the same time, instantly having her body covered, as well.

Covered by a rock-solid, warm body that all but obliterated everything else that existed around her.

Had the air not already been knocked out of her, the pressure, both physical and otherwise, of the detective's firm body against hers would have definitely managed to steal it away.

Wasn't this guy made out of flesh and bone like the rest of them? So why didn't he feel that way?

The thought moved through her startled brain as Kait found herself pinned to the cracked asphalt, unable to draw in a decent breath or proclaim her indignation at being shoved down.

And then came an almost deafening noise right above her head. Three shots fired in rapid succession, sounding so loud, her ears started ringing.

It took Kait a couple of seconds to orient herself amid the chaos and realize that the detective on top of her was the one doing all the shooting.

Opening her mouth to demand that he get off her, she never got the chance to speak.

Tom simultaneously scrambled to his feet, grabbed her forearm and yanked her to standing before dashing over to the fallen thugs, his revolver ready to fire at the first one who moved.

All three were down and bleeding. And cursing a blue streak.

Gun—and eyes—trained on the three men, Tom pulled a handkerchief out of his back pocket and carefully picked up the fallen weapon that was directly in front of the would-be thieves. The weapon that had made him fire his own.

Never once taking his eyes off the suspects, Tom tucked the gun he'd picked up into his waistband. He moved closer to the thugs quickly kicking aside the "slim Jim" one of the would-be carjackers had dropped. The long, thin metal tool was used by thieves, police and car mechanics alike to open up locked car doors when keys were unavailable.

On her feet, tension vibrating through her, Kait took out her own weapon. Not that she thought the detective needed her to back him up. He seemed to be very much in control of the situation. And, she thought with grudging admiration, it looked as if she owed him one. He had, quite possibly, saved her life.

Replaying the scene in her head, Kait realized that she'd heard a crack just as Cavelli had pushed her face down, and the noise hadn't belonged to a dried twig breaking beneath the weight of her foot. One of the thugs had fired in her direction. If this apparently not-so-laid-back detective hadn't acted as quickly as he had, she figured she would have been in a world of hurt right now—if not worse.

Tom turned his head a bare fraction of an inch, just enough for his voice to carry. "Call this in," he instructed.

Behind them, the clerk had wandered out to see what was going on and uttered a mesmerized, "Awesome!" followed by a much more fearful, "Whoa." The latter was accompanied by raised hands as Kait, anticipating more thugs, swung around to aim her weapon at him.

Seeing who it was, Kait frowned and turned back to the three prisoners on the ground.

Her frown deepened. She had no idea what the precinct number was and felt frustrated by her lack of knowledge. Her frustration increased because she had to admit to her ignorance. She'd never liked confessing shortcomings, no matter how minor.

"What do I...?"

Taking a step back so that his line of vision was level with hers, Tom spared a glance in Kaitlyn's direction. He saw that she had her weapon out. Good. He liked that she didn't have to be told to back him up.

Anticipating what she was about to say next, he told her, "Cover them, I'll call the precinct." Tom lowered his weapon just a shade as he pulled out his cellphone.

The man on the ground closest to her had a particularly malevolent expression in his dark eyes. It seemed to mock her. Rocking forward, he looked as if he was starting to get up.

Kait deliberately cocked her revolver, aiming the muzzle straight at him. "Don't even think about it," she told the thug, her voice low, threatening. "I'm not as good a shot as my partner is. If you make so much as a move, I'll shoot. And who knows? I might just hit something important on you. Something you wouldn't want to part with."

Cursing and threatening to get his revenge, the thug nonetheless sank down.

In the middle of requesting a squad car and a couple of paramedics, Tom glanced in Kait's direction. He had caught the offhanded compliment she'd just paid him and smiled to himself. Maybe being paired up with this woman wasn't going to be so bad after all. God knew she was easy on the eyes. If she was good at her job, as well, so much the better.

Finished with the call, Tom tucked away his phone again.

"Go back inside and wait for the paramedics," he told the clerk. The latter quickly vanished. Tom moved in closer to Kait. His eyes swept over her in quick, succinct scrutiny. "You okay?"

"Sure. The shot he got off never hit me," she answered, her eyes still trained on the bleeding threesome, all of whom were on the ground, growing more vocal about their pain, as well as anger over being stopped.

"No, but I did," Tom said. He realized belatedly that in trying to save her, he could have caused her to sustain a concussion. "Sorry I came down so hard on you. I didn't bruise you, did I?"

"Why don't you check her over to make sure?" the man farthest from the front called out and then leered. "Give us something to look at while we're waitin' on that ambulance."

Tom was behind the thug in less than a heartbeat. He grasped the loudmouthed thief by the back of his dark, near-shoulder-length hair and jerked his head back. The thief yelped and then snarled. Tom pulled harder.

"One more word out of you and you're going to have to learn a whole new way to eat your food, because you're not going to have any teeth left." For good measure, he touched just the tip of his gun muzzle to the man's lower jaw. "Do I make myself clear?" he asked in a low voice.

"Yeah," the thief snarled, then stifled a whimper as his hair was drawn back farther. "Perfectly," he uttered between clenched teeth.

"Good." Tom continued to hold on to the man's hair as he ordered, "Now apologize to the lady."

The suggestion was met with rage. "I ain't— Okay, okay," the thug cried as pain shot through his scalp because Tom had pulled harder on the strand of hair he had wound around his fingers. "Sorry," the thief spat out, his small, brown eyes shifting toward Kait. "Didn't mean anything by it."

Kait merely nodded dismissively. She didn't care to hear any insincere apologies. The man was less than dirt to her, anyway. What he said couldn't bother her, couldn't touch her. She'd learned a long time ago how to shut things out, how to compartmentalize.

And, when that failed, how to shut down entirely. There were times when this skill saved her. It kept her from being conquered by the life she'd never asked for and didn't deserve.

The sound of approaching sirens pierced the air, and a squad car arrived just a step ahead of the ambulance that was coming from a different direction.

Tom backed up to let the paramedics and police officers get closer to the prisoners.

"You have some kind of knight-in-shining-armor complex?" Kait asked him.

He assumed she was referring to the interaction with the foulmouthed, would-be thief.

"No complex. I just wanted to teach that lowlife a lesson." When she kept watching him, he elaborated. "That he can't get away with making lewd comments about women in general and especially not about women in the department."

"Technically, I'm not in the department," she pointed out.

His shrug was casual—and oddly sensual, she thought before shutting the thought away. "Minor point," Tom answered.

"That was pretty good shooting," she commented as she attempted to change the subject. He examined her closely, as if he actually *was* checking her over for those bruises he'd asked about. She didn't want him looking at her like that. It didn't make her feel uncomfortable so much as it made her feel…restless. "You get out on the firing range much?"

"Enough." Actually, he went out often. And he *was* good. So good that his name was in the small, select pool the department referred to whenever it needed to put a S.W.A.T. team together. Luckily, that wasn't very often.

But he saw no point in telling her that. Despite the very real seriousness of the situation, the feel of her body beneath his had registered quite acutely. And now that he knew he hadn't injured her, the memory came back for him to dwell on. And savor. It reminded him that it had been quite a while since he'd been out with a woman.

"Cavelli—Cavanaugh," she corrected herself, then stopped. "What do I call you?" she asked. This uncertainty was annoying.

"Tom works," he told her. "Or 'Detective' if you prefer. That hasn't changed any."

Now what was that supposed to mean? What *had* changed? She hated to admit it, but the man had aroused her curiosity, something that was usually dormant as far as she was concerned. For the most part, the only answers she'd ever required were those that directly affected the cases she worked. That had roots in the fact that her distant past was one big, empty space, and because it was, she'd accepted not knowing the answers to a lot of other things. She just wasn't interested in knowing other people's business.

But she had to admit that this mystery surrounding the detective's last name did have her somewhat curious. Why was there a different nameplate on Tom's desk when the chief called him one of his own and referred to him directly by the last name of Cavanaugh?

"Okay," she allowed with a slight inclination of her head. "Tom."

Was she just repeating his name, or drawing his closer attention? He gazed at the woman whose soft contours had momentarily broken through his powers of focus and concentration.

"Yeah?

Kait paused for a moment, looking for words. Expressing gratitude had never been easy for her. She had learned how to shut down early on, and that was her natural state. Warm words were not part of it. Still, the detective had acted quickly and selflessly. She wasn't

the kind to let things like that slide without acknowl-
edgment. "Thanks."

He smiled then, a wide, affable smile, and Kait felt
something strange and unsettling going on in her stomach. And warm. Very warm.

She was driving herself too hard and was probably
coming down with something.

"Glad I was there," Tom told her before heading out
to the front of the building.

So was she, she thought as she followed him.

All three thugs had their wounds—none life-
threatening- -attended to and bandaged. They were
then questioned separately over a number of hours by
both Tom and Kait, acting in tandem and individually.
But after several hours, it became apparent that this was
just a random act. There was no connection between the
theft-gone-bad and the investigation that had brought
her to Aurora in the first place.

The three men weren't kidnappers; they had just
seen an opportunity to steal a vehicle that was a cut
above the rest in the lot. It was just their misfortune
that the car belonged to one of Aurora's finest—and
that their clumsy attempt had been viewed on camera
by another law-enforcement agent.

She was back to square one, Kait thought as she
walked out of the room. An officer was taking the three
down to be booked for attempted auto theft.

Walking back into the squad room, Kait did her
best to keep her disappointment from showing, but she
wasn't as successful as she'd thought.

"Cheer up," Tom coaxed. "Maybe we'll have better
luck with that photo we got off the phony license."

Kait took the photo out of her pocket and unfolded it. The quality of the copy she held was grainy and she didn't hold out too much hope, but right now, it was all she had to go on.

The clerk at the rental agency, once he'd calmed down, had been instructed to call them, night or day, the moment the van was returned to the lot. But there, again, she thought that the chances that they would find anything were slim *if* the van was even returned, which she thought was pretty doubtful. For all she knew, Megan and the van could be halfway across the country by now.

The very thought made her stomach sink. She shut the thought out and looked back down at the paper copy in her hand.

"Who do I see about having this run through facial-recognition software?" she asked.

It was after eight. "There's no one there now, but I'll bring it down to the CSI lab for you," he offered. "They'll get to it first thing in the morning," he promised. The woman looked beat, he noted. Beautiful, but beat. "Want to get something to eat?" he asked.

The thought of eating hadn't even crossed her mind. She shrugged indifferently. "I'll get some takeout on my way out."

"We can get it together," he told her, then explained his offer. "I'm guessing you don't know your way around yet—not that you won't," he interjected quickly before she resurrected the chip to her shoulder. "It's just quicker right now if I take you."

It was on the tip of her tongue to turn down his offer, but if she did she'd be acting too ornery. Even though she wasn't actually hungry, she needed to eat in order to keep going.

"You have a point," she allowed.

"Thanks. I try," he said with a quick, easy smile that, due to her weakened state, she judged, she was finding more and more attractive. "Any kind of takeout in particular you were interested in getting?"

Kait shrugged. Unlike some people who lived to eat, she ate to live. "Food's food," she answered indifferently.

Tom laughed. Andrew Cavanaugh would definitely love to get his hands on her, he couldn't help thinking. The former chief of police who had opted for early retirement to raise his then-motherless five children—and to conduct a long, patient search for the wife he never believed had died when her car went into the lake—had wound up funneling his energy into creative cooking. He made it a point to have everyone in his family—and that included his extended family, otherwise known as the police department—know that his door was always open and that they could always find a hot meal at his table.

Wouldn't he be surprised if one of the members of his newly "uncovered" branch of the family turned up at his table, with a guest no less, Tom mused.

But he wasn't the type to just show up, open invitation or no open invitation. Otherwise, he would have been tempted to bring Kaitlyn to Andrew's house and introduce her to what actual excellent cooking was all about. Him, he couldn't successfully boil water, but that didn't stop him from knowing the difference between a decent meal and one that was just short of heavenly.

Besides, he thought, tired or not she looked as if she

would have his head if he tried to bring her over to Andrew's house.

"Okay." He locked the middle drawer of his desk and stuck the key back into his pocket. It was time to call it a day. "Since you don't really care, if you like pizza I know a place that makes the second-best pizza in Northern California."

She fell into step beside him. "Second best?" she echoed. That was certainly an odd way to put it. "Who makes the first?"

"Andrew Cavanaugh." The man had served up several incredible themes and variations of classic pizza at the last "meeting" that had been called gathering the entire family together.

The man certainly seemed to revel in all that closeness, Tom thought. Up until that point, he'd thought he had a large family when it was just the seven of them and Dad. Now that almost seemed small and cozy in comparison.

"Andrew Cavanaugh," Kait repeated. "Is he any relation to the chief of detectives?"

Tom nodded as he pressed for the elevator. "Andrew's his older brother. He used to be the chief of police," Tom went on, "before he took an early retirement. But that's a long story."

"Another long story," she noted, then asked, "Do all the Cavanaughs have long stories?" She remembered what he'd said earlier about there being a long story behind the discrepancy about his name.

The elevator arrived just as he shrugged. He waited for her to get in, then got in himself. Tom pressed for the first floor. "I don't know. There's a lot of them to ask."

"How many of them are there?" she asked, her curiosity piqued despite her best efforts not to care. "Cavanaughs, not stories," she clarified.

She probably thought he was just carelessly tossing terms around, he thought. Was she in for a surprise. "At last count?"

"Well, yeah."

He paused for a moment, doing a mental head count. He remembered being really overwhelmed when he'd first walked into Andrew's house for the initial introduction, and he wasn't a man who was rattled easily.

Tom suspected that his siblings had all felt more or less the same way. The Cavanaughs en masse were a mighty force to be reckoned with.

"Strictly speaking, if you don't count spouses or children, there are twenty-eight of them—if you include my side of the family."

Kaitlyn stared at him. He had to be pulling her leg. "You're not serious."

"Why wouldn't I be?"

She laughed shortly, shaking her head. "Where I come from, there're towns with less people than that."

He could well believe it. The Southwest had more than its share of small towns. "Yeah, well, fortunately, the Cavanaughs use their powers for good and not evil," he quipped.

Chapter 5

After an initial, mercifully brief discussion as to whether or not they were going to be using two vehicles or just one and if one, which, Tom was a little surprised that he managed to convince Kait that since he actually knew where the restaurant was and she didn't, he should be the one to drive them there.

"I expected you to put up more of an argument," he admitted as he approached his destination several minutes later.

"Didn't really seem worth the effort," Kaitlyn told him.

She had to be tired. But for someone who was obviously dead on her feet, she still looked damn good from where he was sitting.

The restaurant, Naples, had been in the neighborhood for the past thirty-five years. Some said longer.

In that time it slowly expanded from a small, two-table storefront eatery to what it was today, a large, sprawling restaurant that took up a third of the block it was on and was generally filled with customers. Tonight was no exception.

Its patrons didn't seem to mind or really notice that the restaurant's decor amounted to just the bare minimum. The tables all had the classic checkered red-and-white tablecloths, some which were even frayed around the edges. The floor was covered with sawdust that was swept out every night. The prices were more than fair, and what money was left over after the staff was paid went right back into the business. Only the best ingredients were used, and the ovens were top quality. No one had ever been known to go away dissatisfied.

Sitting at the table, waiting for their order to be brought over once it emerged out of the oven, Kait slowly took in her surroundings. She could relate to the bare-bones appearance and rather liked it.

"So, I guess you're not trying to dazzle me," she observed wryly.

"What I'm trying to do is feed you," he reminded Kaitlyn.

From where he was sitting, Tom could easily see the area directly behind the counter where the ovens were situated. The pizza they had ordered—a classic pepperoni with sausage, heavy on the mozzarella—had just been gingerly taken out of the oven. The man who'd prepared it now deftly cut the aromatic pie into equal parts, then loaded his work of art into a large box.

The box in turn was handed over to the waiter who quickly delivered it to their table.

Tom could literally feel his taste buds surfacing and salivating in anticipation of what was ahead. Until he'd tasted Andrew's rendition of pizza, he'd been confident that this place had no match.

It was still an extremely close second.

Throwing open the top of the box, he deposited a slice onto the empty plate in front of Kait, then quickly took one for himself. He savored the first bite like a penitent who'd finally been allowed to enter heaven after an abnormally long wait.

He hadn't had pizza in a week.

"So," he said as he began to feel human again, "where are you staying?"

Busy eating, Kait glanced up at him. She had to admit he was right. Never one who had cared very much for pizza, this could turn her into a true believer.

"Why?" she asked. "Are you planning on standing beneath my balcony and serenading me?"

He supposed, if they worked together long enough, he'd get used to her particular brand of sarcasm. He might even view it as entertaining. Right now, he saw it for what it was. A defense mechanism. He recognized it because he had used the same M.O. on more than one occasion.

"No," he replied easily as he took a second slice out of the box and brought it over to his plate. He noted with satisfaction that Kait was almost finished with her first slice, as well. At least she wasn't pretending not to like it. "I'm just curious if you picked a safe part of the city."

"I come equipped with a gun," she pointed out matter-of-factly. "I'm pretty much safe anywhere." She paused as she took a bite out of a second slice. "But, since you asked—and you are springing for the pizza—right now I'm not staying anywhere." She could see by his expression that her answer aroused a second wave of curiosity, so she indulged him and explained. "I came directly to the precinct when I hit Aurora. I didn't want to waste any time."

She was driven. It didn't take a genius to see that. And it was beginning to have an effect on her. It didn't take a genius to see that, either.

"Just how long has it been since you last slept?" he wanted to know.

About to eat another bite of her slice, Kait lowered it instead and fixed him with a penetrating, reproving look. "What's with all these personal questions, Detective?" she asked.

"Hey, I saved your life," he calmly reminded her. "I figure that entitles me to at least ask a couple of questions about the person I saved."

Kait sighed. She supposed he had a point. Sort of. And she didn't want to come across as completely ungrateful.

"I don't know when I last slept," she admitted grudgingly. "Day before yesterday, I think." Before he could make a comment, she was waving it away. "Don't worry about me. I can get by on very little."

The woman probably thought she was indestructible. But no one was, and since he was, in a manner of speaking, responsible for Kait while she was here, he wanted to make sure she didn't turn into a liability. At the same time, he had a gut feeling that it would be a futile effort to tell her she needed to get some sleep, so he approached the subject in a roundabout way.

"If you haven't gotten a room yet, I've got an extra bedroom if you're interested."

Kait stopped eating. Her eyes met his. Well, that certainly didn't take long.

"I'm not," she informed him firmly.

He realized how she must have misinterpreted his offer. "Not that way," he told her. "Interested as in interested in saving time and money. I'm house-sitting for a friend. The place is located not too far from the precinct, and there's plenty of extra room."

"House-sitting," Kait repeated. That seemed to indicate that he had no place of his own, but she gave him the benefit of the doubt. "All right, where do you normally live?"

Another slice found its way to his plate. "Currently, I'm in between places. The apartment complex I was living in raised its rates. I didn't think the place was worth the price at the lower rent, much less what they raised it to. I was looking for somewhere else to rent when a friend of mine asked me to watch his place while he was away on assignment. He's a photojournalist and his boss was sending him to the Middle East for six months. I said yes and bought myself a little time. I know he wouldn't mind if you crashed there."

Since she was pursuing this case on her own time, all the expenses she was incurring would have to come out of her own pocket. This would be a way to cut a few corners, and it was tempting. Still, she didn't like being in debt to anyone—and she certainly didn't want to be put in a compromising situation if Cavelli took her agreement to mean she was agreeing to other things, as well.

"To be honest, I was actually planning on going back

to the precinct after dinner. I thought I'd start sifting through those surveillance tapes, see if we can get a clearer picture of the guy who rented the van to pass around."

Okay, so maybe the roundabout method wasn't going to work so well in this case. Maybe he needed to be more blunt, Tom decided.

"You'll be of more use to that little girl if you get some decent sleep—something that you won't be getting with your face pressed against a desktop," he assured her. When he saw that she'd started vacillating, he pushed his advantage. "The bedrooms all have locks on the doors and like you've said, you've got a gun," he reminded her. "And if you need any more assurance, I don't believe in mixing business with pleasure."

The last part was an out-and-out lie, but he had a feeling that he wouldn't get her to agree to his offer if she thought he might take advantage of the situation.

Not that she wasn't attractive, but right now, he was more interested in saving that little girl than having a one-night stand, no matter how gorgeous that stand was.

Kait appeared to be mulling it over as she chewed thoughtfully on her third slice of pizza. "I suppose it would be simpler than trying to get a room at a hotel at the last minute—and I hate settling for staying in a motel," she added. Most of the ones that were in her price range were rundown and seedy. And the rooms were little better than oversized bacteria-incubating petri dishes.

Tom did his best not to look triumphant. "All right, we can go straight there whenever you're ready," he told her, nodding at the slice in front of her. It was all but gone at this point.

"We can go straight there *after* we go back to the precinct and I get my car," Kaitlyn corrected him pointedly.

Tom thought of that as an unnecessary step since they were both going to be heading back to the precinct in the morning. He was about to say so when his sixth sense stopped him. She probably saw the car as synonymous with independence. So rather than debate the point, Tom decided that it would be a lot simpler to just agree with her. He coupled his words with a genial smile.

"Whatever you say, Detective."

Rising and picking up the box, he slanted a glance toward Kait. For a moment, he debated saying anything, then decided that he had nothing to lose. The worst that could happen would be for her to tell him to mind his own business.

"Mind if I ask you a question?" he asked as they wove their way out of the restaurant.

She spared him a glance. Was it his imagination, or was that wariness he saw in her eyes? "Go ahead."

"I get the feeling that this case is really important to you."

More probing. Didn't the man ever let up? Was this some kind of a game to him?

"I don't know how it is around here, but a missing little girl isn't something we take lightly back in New Mexico," she informed him tersely.

If she was trying to goad him into losing his temper, she would have to do a lot better than that, he thought. It took more than that to get under his skin.

"We don't take it lightly around here, either," he told her. "But I get the feeling that more is going on here."

She shrugged, looking away. "I can't help what you feel."

He held the door open for her as they walked out. Common sense told him to back away from the subject. After all, this was just a temporary arrangement. With a good dose of luck, they'd find the little girl alive and then the detective with the improbable last name and soul-penetrating eyes would be on her way back to where she'd come from.

And even if the case wasn't resolved to everyone's satisfaction, Two Feathers would still be gone soon enough. There was no reason to trouble himself with the enigmas that she so clearly seemed to represent.

But, for reasons he didn't fathom and—for now — chose not to explore, he didn't want to go on as if it was business as usual. He wanted to understand exactly what was driving her. Was this personal? Did she know the woman whose child had been taken? Had they once been best friends who had lost touch until this horrible tragedy had brought them back in contact?

What, exactly, was it that made this case so personal for her?

And it *was* personal for her. He could see it in her eyes, in the way she conducted herself. Everything about her body language told him that this case was very personal to her.

He was surprised at his own reaction to this. Ordinarily, he wasn't the kind who needed to have answers to everything unless it had to do with a case. But this went beyond that.

"You could try leveling with me," he told her mildly.

The wind had picked up and he turned up his collar to keep it from finding its way down his jacket and along his already chilled spine.

She stopped walking and turned to look at him. Her eyes were blazing. The phrase "beautiful when angry" suddenly popped up in his head. He'd always thought it was a stupid line—until now.

"What is it exactly that you want from me?" she demanded, her voice low but nonetheless heated.

His eyes held hers for a moment and then he studied her face, looking for something he wasn't quite sure of yet. "The truth," he answered without hesitation. "Nothing more."

Kait laughed softly at his words. The laugh had no humor to it.

Nothing more.

Oh, but it was. It was so much more. More than she was willing to talk about, to volunteer. She could hardly bring herself to even *think* about it. Because there was a very real, near-paralyzing chance that that poor little missing girl could even at this very moment be being sold. Sold the way she had almost been sold by a grandmother who was so desperate for a fix, she was half out of her mind and willing to peddle her innocence away to the highest bidder—or any bidder at all.

Kait pressed her lips together. This detective she'd had the misfortune to be paired with wasn't going to back off until she gave him some kind of plausible answer. While it rankled her to be forced to render any sort of an explanation for her actions, Kait reminded herself that he *had* saved her life.

In her book—the book that had been symbolically passed to her by Ronald Two Feathers—that meant she owed him, which in turn dictated that she provide him with answers to whatever questions he had. Just because he asked them.

She took a deep breath and then released it. Braced, she surrendered a fragment, hoping that would satisfy the inquisitive detective and he'd back off. "I promised Megan's mother that I would bring her home by Christmas," she told him quietly.

Tom looked at her for a long moment, hiding his surprise. As cops, they weren't supposed to make promises like that. Promises that in all likelihood they couldn't keep, not through lack of desire or trying but because these kinds of situations never lent themselves to an easy resolution. A promise like that unnecessarily raised hopes and then cut a person's heart out when it fell through.

As if reading his mind, Kait squared her shoulders defensively. "The woman was literally falling to pieces before my eyes and she needed something to hold on to. I gave it to her." In her voice, a host of things went unsaid as her tone challenged him to find fault with what she'd done.

He put a very simple question to her. "What happens when Christmas comes and you're not able to keep your promise?"

Kait drew herself up and raised her chin in what seemed to him to be the most sensual movement he could recall seeing in a very long time. "I don't intend to find out."

The woman had bravado, he'd give her that, Tom thought. It wasn't her ego talking right now, but something else. Exactly what, he wasn't sure yet, but he intended to be along for the ride so that he could find out just what it was.

They'd reached his car by now and he put his key into the lock on the driver's side. Turning it, all four locks sprang open and stood at attention. He opened the rear door directly behind him and placed the half-filled pizza box on the backseat.

Getting in on his side, he buckled up and then waited for her to do the same. After a beat, the detective from New Mexico sank into her seat and then snapped the seat belt harness into place.

"Anything wrong?" he asked as he started up his vehicle.

"No, just reviewing my options."

He slanted her a look. He couldn't help wondering just what sort of options she was reviewing. But when she didn't elaborate any further, he knew it was futile to try to get anything out of her. Maybe she'd be more forthcoming once she trusted him more. He wondered absently how many more times he was going to have to save her life before *that* happened.

"I'll take you back to the precinct," he told her as they hit the main thoroughfare. "Then, once you have your car, if you want to take me up on that offer of using one of the spare bedrooms to crash, you're welcomed to follow me."

She still didn't say anything one way or another. But this time, she smiled.

He took that as a good sign.

When they reached the precinct and he parked next to her dust-covered vehicle—it looked as if she'd brought a part of New Mexico along with her—he still had no idea if she was planning on taking him up on his offer or if she planned to travel another road.

Operating under the assumption that she wasn't going to follow him to his place, when she got out of his car he offered her the contents of the box sitting on the backseat.

"Why don't you take the rest of the pizza with you?" he suggested. "In case you get hungry later on." He began to twist around in order to get a better grasp on the box.

"No," she protested, putting her hand on his arm to stop him. "Leave it where it is." Withdrawing his hand from the edge of the box, he looked at her quizzically. "This way if I lose sight of your car, I'll just follow the aroma, instead."

She probably was just stubborn enough to manage that. But he wasn't about to take any chances. "Why don't I just give you the address?" he suggested, then qualified why he'd said that. "Just in case the wind shifts."

"All right." She waited as he wrote it down, then glanced at the paper he handed her. It looked like a bunch of squiggles square dancing.

When she frowned, Tom wondered if for some reason she had objections to the area. "Anything wrong?"

Squinting at the paper didn't help, either. It was like trying to read hieroglyphics. "You ever consider being a doctor?"

He took a guess as to what was behind her question. "You can't read it?"

Kait shook her head. "Doesn't look like any alphabet I've ever seen."

It wasn't *that* bad, he thought, looking back at the paper himself. He rattled the address off for her. "That says 1551 Monroe Circle."

She examined the paper again, then shook her head. Even with the address now no longer a mystery, she still couldn't see it in what he'd written.

A hint of a smile crept to her lips. "If you say so. Personally, I think I'm better off following the scent of the pizza."

"Whatever works."

But just as he drove up to where she'd left her car, she asked him, "You're sure your friend won't mind you bringing a stranger over to stay at his house?"

"As long as you don't throw a wild frat party while you're staying there, he'll be fine with it." In reality, there wouldn't even be a reason for Matthew, his friend, to even know that anyone else had stayed there.

She stared at him as if he'd just said that he landed from Mars ten minutes ago. "Why would I want to throw a wild frat party?"

"I was being funny," he told her.

There wasn't even a glimmer of a smile on her lips as she said, "If you say so." She got out of his car and glanced at the paper again. "1551 Monroe Circle, huh?" she marveled with another shake of her head. Not a single letter even remotely resembled what he said he'd written. Crumpling the paper, she stuck it into her pocket. "I'll see you there," she promised as she unlocked her own car and got in behind the wheel.

Driving out of the lot, Tom wondered if he'd just made a mistake.

Following close behind him, Kait was wondering the very same thing.

Chapter 6

The house where Detective Tom Cavelli/Cavanaugh apparently lay down his head at night was located in the middle of a residential development that boasted of seven hundred and fifty one- and two-story homes, all huddled together on small lots, none of which was larger than approximately a tenth of an acre. A great many were resting on less than that, bordering on being euphemistically called "patio homes."

Kait couldn't help feeling closed in as she entered the development, following closely behind the other detective's white Crown Victoria. She was accustomed to homes that stood on sprawling pieces of property.

She readily admitted that the houses back home might not be as fancy as what she saw here, but a person could stretch out his or her arms and take a huge breath without accidentally hitting a neighbor in the nose.

She pulled up in the driveway a couple of beats after he had done the same and brought her vehicle to a stop right next to his.

"So, what do you think?" Tom asked, noting the way she was slowly looking around at her surroundings after she had gotten out of her car.

Her first impression was that this was all too rich for her blood. "I think if I lived here and came home to find a car like this next to yours, I'd call the police," she commented honestly.

Her twelve-year-old car, despite the fact that she did baby it, had already had two owners by the time she had gotten to it, and the odometer now had close to two hundred thousand miles on it. While she normally kept it in top running order and incredibly clean, the latter had been a casualty of the road trip she'd taken from her native state to California.

The urgency of the case had made her forget about appearances.

But, confronted with this pristine community, it brought the fact that her roots were from the poorest side of town back to her in glaring lights.

"My friend's not a snob and he's not that shallow," Tom assured her. "And besides, he's not coming home for another couple of months so there's no reason for you to worry about how anyone might react to seeing your car in the driveway."

He didn't bother mentioning that when last appraised, the house had been assessed at over a million dollars. He instinctively knew that would only send her packing to the closest hotel, and she appeared too wiped out to drive down the driveway again, much less out on the main thoroughfare.

"C'mon inside and I'll show you to your room," he urged.

She expected him to open the wide front door with a key and was surprised when the detective paused to punch in numbers on the keypad mounted next to the door frame. Something else they didn't have in her neighborhood. "Your friend's got a security system?"

Tom nodded. "For when he can't get anyone to house-sit," he explained. "He's got a few awards and trophies he's rather partial to and would hate to see stolen." With the alarm disengaged, Tom unlocked the door and held it open for her. "Coming?" he asked when she didn't immediately walk inside.

She offered a tight-lipped smile that had more than a trace of a grimace to it. "Yeah," she responded, coming to life.

She crossed the threshold almost gingerly: Cinderella, not yet in her ball gown, stepping into the palace.

The ground floor was spacious, with high ceilings everywhere and a two-story-tall cathedral ceiling in the living room. The white brick fireplace on the right seemed to extend upward about eighteen feet or so, making her feel incredibly small.

She felt out of place here—but she could definitely get used to it, at least for a few days. As long as she didn't venture out into the postage-size backyard.

"And you're sure your friend won't mind you bringing someone else into his house?" she asked again, still skeptical.

Kait glanced around to see if a security camera was

trained on her. She'd certainly have one if this was her house. She'd have several.

Tom laughed softly to himself. He wouldn't have taken her to be this cautious about crashing somewhere. "I'm sure. We grew up together. He knew exactly who he was giving his house keys and security code to," he assured her.

Kait nodded slowly as his words sank in. "Meaning he knew you weren't going to be a monk." It wasn't a question so much as a realization.

Tom grinned, and she caught herself thinking that it was a nice grin. Probably exactly what he'd intended, she judged.

"Something like that," he agreed delicately. There was no point in elaborating or in saying that he and Matt had more than their share of cruising and hookups when they had first gone to college. "Your room's upstairs," he told her as he headed toward the stairs himself. "C'mon, I'll show you."

Taking the stairs up quickly, Tom paused to wait for her to catch up, then led the way to the second door on his left.

"Mine's right here." He jerked his thumb at the first bedroom on the left. "In case you need anything," he qualified.

Kait took in a breath. God, but she hadn't realized just how tired she was. "I won't," she quickly assured him.

Tom merely nodded, but the grin didn't fade. He gestured toward her room, as if to usher her into it. "All right, then I'll say good-night and just let you get some sleep."

Stepping back from the doorway, he slipped into the

bedroom that his friend used during those short durations when he was actually home. For the most part, he'd seen hotel rooms that had had more of a lived-in look to them than Matt's bedroom did. But then, his friend had always been superneat. Even in college. Which made him the perfect roommate. Matt always kept the area clean.

The house had been closed up all day, keeping in what heat there'd been. Despite the myths about California, Northern California could get really cold at night. There was only a thin comforter on the bed right now, which meant, Tom judged, that his houseguest was probably going to need a blanket beside the comforter.

He remembered seeing a couple of extra blankets stacked at the top of the closet in the master bedroom he was using. Pushing the sliding door to one side, he found what he was looking for. There were actually three blankets, all in varying shades of blue. Matt's favorite color, Tom recalled.

Taking the one on top, a royal-blue blanket made out of fleece, Tom pulled it down and went to offer his prize to Kait.

Coming out of his room, he was surprised to see that she hadn't closed her door yet. Had she gone downstairs to get something from her car?

But when he peered into the second bedroom, he saw that not only was the detective from New Mexico in the bedroom, she was lying on the bed, on top of the comforter, out like the proverbial light. He could only guess that she must have either been more tired than she'd been willing to admit, or that she'd decided to test out the quality of the mattress and had fallen asleep during the process.

Approaching the bed, he looked at his guest more closely. She didn't seem nearly as tough asleep as she did awake. But the reason for the transformation was because, asleep, her face was relaxed rather than pensively frowning.

He was about to quietly retrace his steps and leave the room but then he hesitated, debating. The temperature would still fall lower tonight, and Two Feathers *was* lying on top of the bedding.

Moving into the room even more slowly, he was as silent as a shadow. As silent as she probably was capable of moving. Very carefully, Tom unfolded the blanket he had and then spread it out over her.

Kait stirred unexpectedly just then, but her eyes continued to be shut. Tom slowly let out the breath that had gotten caught in his throat the moment she began to move. More than likely, she was just getting herself into a better position on the bed. She was still asleep, he concluded, relieved.

"You don't look so tough now, Detective Two Feathers," he whispered softly.

Two Feathers. If it was the last thing he did, he would get her to explain that name to him. He'd bet a year's salary that this woman was a genuine redhead. Her hair was that reddish/strawberry blond shade that only true redheads tended to have, and as far as he knew there were no redheads in any of the Native American tribes.

So was she pulling his leg, or was her surname actually Two Feathers? He was fairly convinced that the police department would have uncovered any aliases before this.

Satisfied that she would stay warm enough, Tom went back to his own room. He took off his shoes and stripped off his shirt. His pajamas of choice were a pair of jeans that were all but worn out.

He was bone weary himself now that he thought of it. Tom got into bed and turned off the lamp on the nightstand.

It was the last thought that crossed his mind. He was out the second his head hit the pillow.

The noise woke him before he could place it or decide whether it originated in his dream, or was coming from somewhere outside the house.

A second after he sat up, listening, Tom realized that it was neither. The whimpering cry hadn't been a vivid part of his dream nor was it coming from somewhere outside the house.

It was coming from somewhere *inside* the house.

He cocked his head, trying to place where the sound was coming from. Brimming with sadness, it had almost a keening quality to it.

Even as the sound teased his brain, Tom was on his feet, making his way to his closed door in bare feet. Once he opened his bedroom door, he could hear the sound more clearly.

He also placed it instantly.

It was coming from the next room. From Kait's room. It sounded like a cross between a whimper and a cry. His first thought was that someone had broken in, but that wasn't possible. The alarms would have gone off. He'd armed the system himself.

He'd left Kait's door opened when he'd slipped out earlier so there was no need to stand on ceremony, debating whether or not he should go in.

He went in.

And found that she was still sound asleep. But she

was definitely the one making that soul-wrenching noise. Something within the nightmare she was so obviously having frightened her. Badly.

"Two Feathers, wake up. It's okay." His urgent words had absolutely no effect. She was still asleep, still suffering.

He'd once heard that it wasn't good to wake a sleepwalker, but the woman wasn't moving, just crying out, and her cries got louder, along with the level of her distress.

Tom tried waking her up by shaking her shoulder. His first attempt was gentle, but when that had no effect, he shook her harder.

Kait screamed outright, her eyes still shut and she remained asleep.

At that point, Tom went with his gut instincts. He sat down on the edge of the bed and did his best to take her into his arms as he called her name over and over again.

Still asleep, Kait started swinging, trying to break free of the hold he had on her. She was as frightened and as angry as he could ever remember seeing.

Doggedly, he continued holding on to her. "Kait, Kait, it's all right. You're safe. You're here and you're safe. For God's sake, wake up. It's just a nightmare. Nothing more than a nightmare, you hear me?" He kept repeating the words over and over again in a firm, soothing voice.

Finally, he got through to her.

Her eyes flew open. For a fleeting moment, she seemed to slump against him, clinging to him as if he was her life preserver. But then her body became rigid as she pulled back.

She looked disoriented and still very, very frightened.

"What are you doing?" she demanded angrily, yanking against him.

She tried to break free of his hold and found to her horror that his grip was much too strong for her to break.

Just like *his* had been.

The second she thought that, Kait broke out in a cold sweat. She could feel it, feel fear trickling down her spine, pooling at her waist.

Snap out of it! You're not ten years old anymore. You're not that defenseless little girl. You're a cop now, a detective. There's a gun in the nightstand drawer. Your gun.

All she had to do was reach it.

"I'm trying to keep you from knocking all my teeth out," Tom told her. Holding on to her was like trying to hang on to a bucking mustang. Any second now, she would break free. He had to let go before that, otherwise who knew what she would think? "Okay, I'm letting go," he announced, raising his hands up in the universal sign of surrender. "Take a deep breath, Detective. You're safe. It was just a nightmare. One hell of a nightmare," he added, shaking his head. "But still just a dream."

Taking a deep, ragged breath, Kait dragged a hand through her hair as she looked around the room. The lamp wasn't on, but light streamed in from the hallway.

Slowly, she exhaled and struggled to relax as she realized that she'd been dreaming. And then she looked at the man still sitting on the edge of the bed.

Her eyes narrowed a little. "What are you doing in here?" she asked, but the anger, the fear was all but gone from her voice. All that remained was a leery woman who wanted explanations.

"I heard you crying. You were so loud, you woke me up," he told her truthfully. There was concern in his voice as he asked, "What were you dreaming about?"

Kait stifled a shiver. The last thing she wanted to do was talk about the dream, talk about her past. It had taken a great deal for her to put her own head right. To struggle and manage to put her demons to rest all on her own without enlisting anyone's help. Even so, she had a feeling that Ronald had known. She had a hunch that was why he'd stepped up the adoption process, started the day he'd gotten married. He had been determined to pull her out of the system before it ate her alive. Luckily, he'd married an understanding woman.

Luck, she'd often thought, actually didn't have anything to do with it. Though he loved her, he would have never married Winona if she hadn't agreed to starting a family by taking in a twelve-year-old, emotionally scarred child.

Because Tom was still looking at her, waiting for an answer, she shrugged. "Doesn't matter."

"You almost took my head off," he pointed out mildly, and then grew more serious as he added, "and you were really terrified. I know the difference, and I think it does matter."

She struggled to curb her impatience. "Look, thank you for waking me up, but it's nothing. Really," she insisted with feeling. "It was just a bunch of random things—I can't even remember what I was dreaming about anymore," she said matter-of-factly. With another half shrug she told him, "Dreams fade once you're awake. You know that."

He'd be willing to bet a year's salary that hers hadn't. They were still very much a part of her.

"You ever shake a bottle of soda?" he asked without preamble.

Kait stiffened. "No, I haven't," she answered pointedly, her tone telling him to back off.

She should have known better. He might look laidback, but it was obvious that Tom-with-the-two-lastnames was as dogged as she was.

"Well, when you shake a bottle of soda," he continued, his voice still deceptively mild, "the pressure inside starts to build. Sometimes, even if you don't take off the top yourself, the built-up pressure gets so bad that what's inside the bottle explodes anyway, sending the bottle cap flying off through the air like some kind of a missile, even shattering the bottle in the process. All that could have been avoided—"

Her eyes met his, daring him to contradict her. "If you never shook the bottle in the first place."

He wasn't about to get bested that easily. "Or, barring that," he continued amiably, "if you released the pressure slowly by lifting the bottle cap just a crack at a time."

Her eyes narrowed again, this time pinning him to where he sat. "If you're thinking of lifting my top, the answer's no," she informed him, enunciating each word carefully.

The so-called warning inadvertently brought a smile to his lips. He hadn't meant the word "top" in the way she indicated, and he had more than a passing hunch that she knew that. Maybe she wanted to create a mental diversion, and for a second he had to admit that she'd succeeded. The words conjured up an image in his mind that had nothing to do with nightmares and everything to do with the woman sitting up in bed beside him.

Her hair was a wild red storm about her face and Kait was still breathing heavily, her chest reverberating with every breath she drew in and released.

Creating wild fantasies in his head that had no business being there.

Nonetheless, there they were.

"Just trying to help, that's all," he managed to offer up in his own defense.

She knew he was, but in order for him to help, she'd have to let him in. Have to allow him access to the world of unspeakable pain she had endured while in the system, being passed around from one family to another.

She was supposed to be over that by now, and most of the time she was. But when she ran into cases like the one she was presently handling, the nightmares came back, and then suddenly she was reliving those awful days. In the blink of an eye, she was ten years old again. Having things happen to her that no ten-year-old should ever have to endure.

"It was just a stupid dream," she assured him again. "Thanks again for waking me up."

"Yeah, sure," he said with a shrug. He'd interviewed more than his share of people to know that he wasn't going to get anything more out of her tonight. He might as well just get back to sleep.

Tom began to rise, then changed his mind. He glanced at the woman who had aroused his sympathy even though he knew if he mentioned it, she'd most likely force-feed that sympathy back to him, not necessarily through his mouth.

"Want me to stick around until you fall asleep?" he suggested.

"Now why would I want that?" There was a heavy dose of sarcasm in her voice.

"When my younger sister used to have nightmares, she'd have trouble getting back to sleep unless I stayed with her until she dropped off. She said it made her feel better. Nothing wrong with wanting to feel better. We all want that."

Kait shrugged. "It's up to you. You want to stick around, playing Prince Charming to my Sleeping Princess, it's up to you. But like I said, I'm fine," she informed him firmly.

He noticed she'd said "Sleeping Princess" instead of the standard term, "Sleeping Beauty," and wondered if it had been deliberate or just an error because she was tired.

"Never said you weren't," he answered.

Nonetheless, he stayed where he was until she finally dropped off to sleep. And then he lingered a little while longer. Just in case the nightmare returned.

Chapter 7

"**W**ho was holding on to you?"

It was the next morning and he and Kait had just arrived in the precinct's parking lot. As he had anticipated, Kait had driven in her own vehicle.

Since having the car easily accessible seemed to mean so much to the woman and obviously represented independence to her, he hadn't tried to talk her into leaving it in his driveway. After the incident in her room last night, he knew that despite her bravado, a fragile woman lived beneath the tightly wrapped layers.

He also suspected that she would continue to keep that fragile side buried rather than try to find a way to heal.

It was early, earlier than he was accustomed to coming in. But Kait was chomping at the bit to begin viewing the tapes and capture a better close-up of the man who had rented the van used in the abduction. Since the chief of Ds had unofficially made the visiting detective his responsibility, Tom knew that he couldn't just let her come back to the precinct without him. No matter how much he wanted to get some extra shut-eye to make up for what he'd lost playing her human night-light last night.

Beauty sleep would just have to wait.

About to walk up the back steps into the building, Kait abruptly stopped dead and looked at him quizzically. Her guard was up as she asked, "What?"

"When you were having that nightmare last night, you were begging someone to let you go," he said. "Who was it that you thought was holding on to you?"

He watched her stiffen, as if she was bracing for a physical blow.

"The devil."

The answer was flippant, but in this case, it actually fit the situation, she thought. Because the foster parent so vividly conjured in her nightmare had been more devil than human when she'd had to live with the man and his wife. The moment she became a police-woman, she'd gone back to the house where she had spent a hellish five months. She'd been prepared to do whatever it took to arrest the man as well as his wife and bring them up on charges of child endangerment and molestation.

At the time, it was too late to bring her own case to light. The statute of limitations had run out on that. But she was positive that hers hadn't been an isolated inci-dent. There had to have been more little girls who had suffered at Elliot Caulfield's hands.

But life had cheated her again. Her former foster

parents were both dead thanks to a murder/suicide that had taken place in their house less than a year earlier.

Coming away from the neighborhood, she'd felt both vindicated and disappointed at the same time. She'd been struggling to put the memory behind her and had thought she'd succeeded.

But this case had brought it all back to her. Just her luck, the Aurora detective had been a witness to her unintentional meltdown.

"I already told you, I don't remember," she insisted, then went on the offensive. "Didn't you ever have dreams that faded the second you were awake?"

"Yeah." His tone of voice told her that whether or not he'd had those kind of dreams was beside the point. In this case, he didn't believe her. She knew that what he believed or didn't believe shouldn't bother her. But it did.

You've got something more important to focus on, remember? Kait upbraided herself. *Megan needs you.*

"Let's go watch those surveillance tapes and see if we can get a better shot of the man who rented that van," she urged.

Turning her back on Tom, she raced up the stairs.

Finding their quarry on the rental-agency tapes turned out to be a great deal more difficult than they'd originally thought. Whether due to a power failure or plain neglect and incompetence, the clock on the recording camera hadn't been set correctly so the time stamp on the tapes was off, not by hours but by days.

Consequently, finding the man they searched for wasn't just a matter of queueing up the tape to the approximate time he had rented the vehicle. They were left to painstakingly go through all the tapes they'd collected to identify the man who had driven off with the white van. At the very least, with both of them diligently working, it would take at least hours if not the whole day.

"Damn it!"

Sequestered in an almost claustrophobically small, darkened video room where they had been sitting side by side, Tom's head shot up when he heard Kait bite off the curse. He realized belatedly that he'd almost nodded off from boredom.

Looking at her monitor now, he searched the screen, trying to see what had prompted that reaction from her. "You find him?"

The triumph she'd anticipated when she finally located the son of a bitch who had taken Megan was pointedly missing.

"Yeah, I found him," she grumbled.

"What's the matter?" he asked.

"Look at him!" she cried, waving her hand angrily at the screen. "He's wearing a ski jacket with the collar turned up and a hat. All he's missing is a ski mask." She suppressed the second curse that rose to her lips. "He could be anybody," she said in disgust. "For all we know, that could be a woman or even a dog trained to walk on its hind legs."

He could understand her frustration, but something could be gleaned from the segment. "Hold on, now. Rewind that. We might not have a clear shot of his face, but maybe we can pick up something else from the clip."

Her eyes narrowed as she dared him to find something positive from this. "Like what?"

"Rewind the tape to just before he opens the back door to the lot," Tom instructed.

Frowning, she did what he asked even though she thought it was a huge waste of time. When she'd rewound it to just before the man emerged from the rear of the building to claim the van he'd requested, she hit Play.

"Slower," he told her. "Play that in slow motion," he added, watching her screen intently.

"What are you looking for?" Kait asked.

"Something. Anything." His eyes remained trained on the monitor, straining to catch the one telltale detail that might put their search into the proper perspective. "I'll know it when I see it."

"Terrific," she muttered under her breath. In other words, he hadn't a clue.

Trying to work her way past the encroaching hopeless feeling, Kait rewound the tape a third time. When she played it this time, it advanced a frame at a time. Kait stared at the screen, hating that she didn't see what the other detective apparently was looking for.

"You getting anything out of this?" Kait finally asked.

There were tiny bits and pieces of information. If put together, would they be larger than the sum of their parts? He had no answer, but he knew he had to play every angle. They were all that missing little girl had.

"Well, he's a short man," Tom told her.

He looked to be of average height to her. "How can you tell?"

Tom hit the pause button and the video froze the man on the screen in an awkward position. "Look where his shoulder comes up to against that poster on the back wall," he pointed out, tapping the screen. "When we were out in the lot, I looked down at the poster. The kidnapper had to look up to see it." She'd begun advancing the film again. "There!" he cried. "Freeze it." When Kait did, he ran his finger along the man's basic outline. "He also either has a limp or one leg is just a little shorter than the other, because his gait is uneven," he told her with finality.

She'd been so intent on getting a clearer picture, she hadn't even paid attention to the way the man moved. From side to side like some roly-poly clown doll.

"Wow, Ronald would have been impressed with you." To her, that was the highest compliment she could bestow on anyone.

"Ronald?" Was that the name of a boyfriend? Tom couldn't help wondering. Someone she'd left back home she needed to get back to? And why did the identity of this "Ronald" person pique his curiosity so much?

She nodded. "My father."

Rather than answer questions, the revelation only raised more. "You call your father by his first name?" He found that a little odd.

A bittersweet mood moved over her, taking her emotions prisoner. "Right now, I'd call him anything he wanted if he was just around to answer." She saw the question rise to the other detective's eyes. "He died four years ago." He'd lived just long enough to see her made the youngest detective in the precinct. He'd been so proud of her. "Best man to ever walk the earth," she said with no little feeling.

"I'm sorry for your loss."

It never ceased to strike him how very hollow those words sounded even when he meant them in all sincerity. The words, the sentiment behind them, didn't begin to embrace the immense sorrow he knew that the loss of a parent or someone close had to generate. When his mother had succumbed to an insidious disease, the hole left in his family's hearts had been insurmountable.

"Really," he added with quiet fierceness.

Her eyes met his for a moment. The flip comment that automatically came to her lips faded before she could give voice to it.

Instead, she told him, "I believe you. And I called him by his first name because I first knew him as 'Uncle Ronald.'" She could see more questions forming in his mind. Maybe it did deserve an explanation. She wasn't ashamed of her connection to Ronald. "I was about three or four at the time. He and his partner posed as a couple desperate to adopt a baby. I remember just before they came, my grandmother warned me that if I wasn't nice to these people and they left without me, she'd stick a hot poker into my mouth to show me what happened to 'bad little girls who didn't listen to their grandmother.' I remember being so scared," she admitted. "Then there was a lot of commotion and there were all these policemen, handcuffing my grandmother and her boyfriend and taking them away. I started to cry. What I remember most of all were these big, strong arms lifting me up."

She pressed her lips together as she remembered and relived the moments. "He told me everything was going to be okay."

"And was it?" Tom asked. He studied her as she answered. Maybe this would give him more of a handle on the woman he was being paired with.

"No, but not because Ronald broke his word to

me," she said defensively. "Family court put me into the system and I got passed around to whatever foster family would take me at the time."

Tom watched the corners of her mouth curve ever so slightly in what had to be one of the saddest smiles he'd ever seen. "Ronald would always find me and come visit. He'd bring me food, or new clothes. Once he brought me a hairbrush because my hair was so knotted." Fondness slipped into her voice as she recalled the incident. "He spent two hours trying to get the knots out without hurting me. Finally, I had to have my hair cut. I looked like a boy. He promised it would grow out and got me a hat to wear until it did."

Her words echoed back to her. Startled, she stared at Tom. Her tone changed abruptly. "How did you do that?" she asked.

"Do what?"

It was too late to pull back. The damage had been done. She'd let him see her vulnerable side. "How did you manage to wheedle that out of me?"

"I didn't wheedle anything," he told her calmly. "I just listened to you talk." His eyes were kind as they held hers. "You were the one who volunteered all that information. I didn't twist your arm."

Kait pressed her lips together. She wasn't about to beg, and she knew that a threat was out of place here. Annoyed and flustered with herself, all she could do was appeal to his sense of honor.

"I'd appreciate it if you kept what I just told you to yourself."

She was lucky that LaGuardia hadn't been within earshot, Tom thought. The other man had a terrible penchant for not being able to keep secrets.

"Wasn't planning on having it pop up on my Facebook page."

Her eyes widened.

"I'm just kidding." Tom bit his lower lip as he struggled not to laugh at the look on her face. "I was just being flippant." He looked at her pointedly. "It's a habit I seemed to have picked up just recently."

Kait released the breath she'd been holding. "Point taken." And then she mumbled a near inaudible, "Thanks," before asking him in a louder voice, "So now what do we do?"

"We go back to the fake driver's license and take the photo we found there down to the tech lab to see if they can match it up with a face that is actually *on* a real California driver's license." Turning his monitor and the ancient VCR off, Tom rose to his feet.

Kait was already moving toward the door.

When she opened it, she was forced to squint at the brightness of the light coming in from the hall. She held her hand up before her eyes to help.

"I had no idea the lights in the hall were so bright." Very slowly, she raised her eyelids, trying to acclimate herself to the light.

"Now I know how that gopher feels, popping his head out of that hole in February," Tom commented. He closed the door to the windowless room behind him.

"Groundhog," she corrected, wishing she'd thought to bring her sunglasses with her.

The word had been half grunted, half mumbled. He wasn't sure he'd heard her right. "What?"

"It's a groundhog, not a gopher," she told him, enunciating more clearly. "That's why it's called 'Groundhog Day,' not 'Gopher Day.'"

He inclined his head, accepting her correction. He had a feeling she didn't tolerate being wrong. The woman was undoubtedly very hard on herself. "I stand corrected."

She slanted a look at his face, trying to discern if he was having fun at her expense. Apart from Ronald and his wife, forming any sort of a relationship had always been difficult for her.

"You're humoring me, aren't you?" she asked suspiciously.

"I doubt if that's possible." He had a feeling she handed people their heads for that, because she probably took it as their making jokes at her expense. "What I was just doing was admitting that I was wrong. I do that on occasion," he told her. "If I'm wrong," he underscored. Then, changing the subject, he urged, "C'mon, the sooner we get someone started on that facial-recognition program, the sooner we might come up with an actual name for this guy."

The fact that they hadn't already taken the fake copy with its fuzzy photograph to the lab was on her, Kait thought, annoyed with herself. She'd held off because she'd hoped they would come up with a clearer, more focused photograph than the overexposed one that the rental agency had copied for their files.

"Yeah," she agreed, lengthening her stride to keep up with the detective again. "I've already wasted too much precious time."

She fervently prayed that this play for time wouldn't cost Megan her life—or have her disappear out of sight forever.

As they approached the elevator, Tom looked at the intense detective, and he could almost read her thoughts. He *had* to find a way to get her to lighten up. Otherwise she would self-combust on him.

"Do you always beat yourself up this much?" he asked.

He could see that his question had ticked her off. That wouldn't have been his first choice for a reaction, but he'd take it. Being annoyed at him restored her fighting spirit, which was what he was trying to accomplish in the first place.

"Where is this lab?" she asked.

The elevator arrived just then and he waited for her to get in before getting on himself. When he did, he pushed the button labeled B.

"Guess," he said. A smile played on his lips as he said it. One that she could only describe as seductively mischievous.

Too bad she was immune to that sort of thing, she thought.

"The basement," she answered with impatient annoyance. Why was he playing games? And why was that smile of his causing this odd sensation to sprout and grow in the pit of her stomach?

"Very good." As they rode down, Tom inclined his head as if he was bowing to her superior intellect. "You got it on the first guess."

Kait instantly resented his frivolous tone. A little girl's life was at stake. Didn't he get that? Or didn't he care? She wasn't sure which was a worse offense, stupidity or indifference.

"Why aren't you taking this seriously?" she demanded heatedly.

He could see where this was going, and he didn't care for it. He wasn't just a fairly decent detective, he was a damn good one. That meant he cared. More than he actually should at times.

"I am."

Kait laughed shortly. "By making lame jokes?" she challenged.

Tom debated just letting the accusation hang in the air without answering it. To the undiscerning eye, he might appear laid-back, but he didn't like having to explain himself and he certainly didn't like to justify his actions. Especially not to his partner. A partner was supposed to have your back even if it was a matter of blind faith.

And, for better or for worse—and for the duration of this case—this woman was his partner. He might need her to have his back. Especially if they wound up stumbling on a kidnapping ring. And if that did happen, then alienating her now wouldn't be such a wise move.

So he told her the truth. He told her why, at times, especially when all else might fail, humor ended up being his weapon of choice.

"By not allowing my outrage, my sense of horror and my anger at the lowlife who would rip an innocent child from her family to get to me to the point that I am almost paralyzed and utterly useless when it comes to working a case." And then he attempted to lighten the mood by adding, "And the jokes aren't lame. They're just not overly clever."

No one had gotten on or off, so they had ridden the elevator straight to their destination. The elevator doors opened as the car arrived in a corner of the basement.

"They're lame," Kait insisted, but this time, he saw that there was just a hint of a smile on her lips, as well as one that he could just make out distantly in Kait's voice.

Tom silently congratulated himself. However minor, he was making headway.

Chapter 8

Ever since the bombshell had dropped into his world that he was not the son of the late Martha and Anthony Cavelli but was actually born into what had slowly transformed into the Cavanaugh dynasty, Sean Cavelli/Cavanaugh was forced to wrestle with a number of issues, including the so-called "simple" act of selecting which surname he was legally supposed to be using.

For more than five decades, he'd thought of himself as Sean Cavelli, a man whose relatives on both sides of the family had their roots in Italy. Never mind that he didn't resemble either of his parents or any of his three siblings.

Currently, he could truthfully admit that he wasn't quite comfortable with either last name.

Still, as Thomas, his oldest son, had pointed out to him the first time they'd discussed this unexpected twist in their lives, he was still the same person he'd been before the discovery had been unceremoniously dropped on all of them. He still had the same abilities and insights, still had the background and training for the profession he both loved and did so well. Just because the letters of his last name had changed—and not even his initials, he thought, amused—that didn't diminish his previous accomplishments or minimize anything he would do from here on in.

He was still the same person, and whether that person was Italian or Scottish or some other ethnic nationality would not ultimately change anything.

Sean carefully separated the fragments of a shredded garment he'd been given to work with this morning in the hopes that he would be able to extract some DNA from the fibers. He worked slowly, methodically, the way he always did.

Sometimes wisdom didn't come with age, he thought with a smile. Sometimes it was there all along, as in Thomas's case. Unlike some of the others, this revelation about the hospital's mix-up didn't seem to faze his oldest son in the least.

"Speak of the devil," Sean said as he looked up and saw his son and a woman he didn't recognize walking into the lab.

Tom looked around. For once the lab appeared to be empty, except for his father, who headed up the crime-scene-investigation day unit. It had been his father's recent transfer from a neighboring forensic lab that had started the whole identity-discovery process in the first place.

"There's no one here. Just who were you speaking of the devil to?" Tom asked, amused.

"Just thinking out loud," Sean answered dismissively. "Never mind that, what did you bring me?" As he asked, Sean looked at the attractive, very serious-looking redhead behind his firstborn.

Tom stepped to the side and gestured toward the detective with him. "This is Detective Kaitlyn Two Feathers. The case she was working on in New Mexico led her to Aurora, so here she is." He held up the copy of the driver's license photo they'd lifted out of the rental car agency's files. "Do you think you can run this photograph through the facial-recognition program and find a name for us?"

Sean looked at the reproduced photograph dubiously. He noticed that, as with all state licenses, there was a name and address next to the photograph. "The one on here isn't good enough?" he asked.

"It's a fake," Tom told him. "And so is the address."

"And he has such an honest face, too," Sean bemoaned wryly. He studied the reproduction and frowned. The picture was fuzzy at best. "This is the clearest photo you have of him?"

"It's the *only* one we have of him," Kait answered before Tom could. Sean gathered that the detective from New Mexico was not happy about that.

Sean took the information in stride. In general, he tended to be optimistic, even when the outlook was bleak. "Well, something is always better than nothing. I'll see what I can do with this and give you a call later. Sooner if something comes up," he promised. He began to put the sheet at the bottom of his considerable pile of work. "What's he done?" he asked, mildly curious about a case that would have a detective crossing state lines.

There was restrained anger in Kait's voice as she answered. "He abducted a little girl from in front of her house while she was playing with her friends."

Sean didn't comment on the information. He pulled the copy back out from the bottom of the pile and then placed it on top. Cases involving children always got his immediate attention. Someone had to champion the innocent.

"I'll be in touch," he promised with feeling.

"You've got all the numbers," Tom replied as he turned away and left the lab.

"Think he'll actually get to that today?" Kait asked, glancing over her shoulder back at the lab.

"Yeah, I do," Tom assured her as they walked down the less than brightly lit hallway back toward the elevator. "My father has a personal vendetta against anyone who harms a kid."

Kait stopped dead and looked at him as his words sank in. "Wait. That tall man in the white lab coat, that was your father back there?"

"He's my father out here, too," Tom teased. He could see that his quip had eluded her. She was preoccupied, so he sobered slightly as he repeated, "Yeah, that's my father."

"Why didn't he say something? Why didn't *you* say something?" Kait wasn't sure exactly why, but she felt like an idiot who'd been shut out and wound up standing awkwardly on the outside of a joke.

"For the same reason Dad's not sure what last name he wants to use from here on in, Cavelli or Cavanaugh. He believes in being professional, in relying on not who he knows but *what* he knows. That's why, when we're here, I'm not his son, I'm the detective from Missing

Persons. And he's not my father, he's the head of the CSI lab, day shift.

"As it is," Tom continued as he resumed walking to the elevator, "a lot of the Cavanaughs are always being accused of nepotism, either in the way they got a promotion or in the way someone in their family got one. It's very important to Dad that he—and the rest of us working at the precinct—rely on merit and not connections." Stopping in front of the elevator, Tom pushed a button for the car. "Dad's integrity means a lot to him. He doesn't want anyone to think that he got to be head of the lab because the chief of Ds is his long-lost brother. He actually became the head of the lab before any of us even knew there *was* a mix-up."

"Hold it—back up," Kait said. "*What* mix-up?"

He'd gotten so used to everyone knowing the story that he'd forgotten that some people didn't. "Seems that when my dad was born, there was another little boy in the same hospital on the same day. Somehow the names accidentally got mixed up and my dad was taken home by the Cavelli family, while his real family, the Cavanaughs, took home the baby they thought was theirs. That baby died, and my father thrived. The mix-up only came to light a few months ago. We've all been adjusting to it since then."

"Wow." It was the only word that seemed to fit there.

"Yeah. Wow," he agreed.

Kait couldn't help wondering if there were other babies out there who had gotten accidentally switched. In her case, it wasn't even something she could remotely hope for. She'd been born behind bars, when her mother was serving time. From her limited information, there had been no one to get switched with.

The last baby in the prison hospital had been born six months before her.

The elevator arrived and they got on. Tom pressed the button corresponding to their floor.

"How long have you known about this mix-up?" she asked him.

In a way it felt as if he'd just found out yesterday. In another, it was as if he'd known about this forever. The truth was found somewhere in between.

"Just a few months," he admitted. "Four, if you want a number."

For just a moment, Kait tried to put herself in the other detective's position. What if she suddenly discovered that her parents had been important people in the community instead of a dead, small-time thief and his junkie girlfriend? Most likely, she'd probably feel excited—and cheated at the same time. Cheated because she'd been passed around as a child and had missed out on being treated like a human being.

But Ronald did his best to make that all up to you, remember? And the minute he could adopt you, he did. If you'd had a normal background, you might never have met Ronald. And you would have been poorer for it.

She realized that Tom was watching her because she'd suddenly grown so silent. She didn't want him asking her any questions, so she asked him one instead. "How do you feel about being a Cavanaugh?"

"Not sure yet," he admitted honestly. "They cast long shadows and there's a lot to live up to."

"Afraid you can't?" she asked. He didn't strike her as the insecure type.

"Blunt," he acknowledged. "You don't beat around the bush, do you?"

"What's the point?" she challenged. "You don't find things out that way and what happens is that you get left with a lot of unanswered questions."

"All right, to answer your question." Tom obliged. "No, I'm not afraid that I won't be able to live up to their reputation. I do pretty good work and I'm comfortable in my own skin."

He certainly seemed that, she thought. "That puts you up on a lot of people."

He looked at her for a long moment and then asked, "On you?"

She laughed shortly. "Now who's being blunt?"

Reaching their floor, the elevator stopped and its doors opened. He gestured toward her, giving her the credit as he said, "I learn from the best."

Smooth, she thought. "And who taught you how to flatter like that?"

"I came by that naturally," he told her.

He'd probably be surprised that she took his words to heart as a warning. Because he had a way about him, she'd already learned that. A way of being able to extract information out of her, of having her tell him things she'd had no intentions of owning up to. By working his black magic, he'd learned more about her in a little less than two days than most people she worked with on the force back in New Mexico had in the six years she'd been there.

But that was because she kept to herself for the most part. That wasn't as easy to do here around Cavelli/ Cavanaugh or whatever he wanted to call himself.

She walked back to her temporary desk, promising herself she was going to be more vigilant. And silent.

The rest of the day was spent going around in circles. At least that was how it felt when she was about to call it a night and leave the precinct. The reprint of the fake driver's license hadn't yielded a match so far from the databases that Sean had accessed.

A call to the clerk back at the car-rental agency had proved to be equally fruitless. The van hadn't been returned. The contact number that had been left in the file got them nowhere, as well.

The moment she pressed the last digit on the landline keypad, Kait heard a teeth-jarring, high-pitched noise screeching out of the receiver.

She winced as she pulled it away from her ear. Suppressing a few choice words she had for the clerk at the rental agency, she dropped the receiver back into the cradle with a resounding noise.

"What *was* that?" Tom asked, his own teeth set on edge just from the echo of the noise.

"Apparently the guy who abducted Megan left a fax number with the rental agency. What?" she asked when she saw the sudden alert look that came into the other detective's eyes.

"Whenever my sister Bridget orders something online and she doesn't want to give out her home number, she uses the old fax number she had while she was working for a temp agency when she was still in college. She never got around to getting rid of it. Maybe the guy we're after does the same thing."

She didn't see where this was going. "Okay…" she drew out, waiting for him to fill in more.

"My point is that maybe the number's connected to the guy somehow. A fax line he maintains for some professional reasons." He shrugged. The reason was unimportant, as long as the number was traceable. "It's worth exploring," he urged. "What's the number?"

Instead of rattling it off, Kait handed him the piece of paper with the number that she'd scribbled down yesterday on it. "Here."

He was already on his feet. "I'll run it down," he told her.

Maybe being around him challenged her to think harder. Whatever the reason, ideas had begun popping up in her brain. "Wait a second. I just thought of something."

He heard the excitement in her voice and turned to face her. "Go ahead."

Her eyes were shining as she took him into her thought process. "The guy who abducted Megan had to sign some papers agreeing to the fees and all that stuff when he originally rented the van."

He knew where she was going with this. The same thought had just occurred to him. "And he had to have handled the paper when he handed it back to the clerk."

"Which means his fingerprints have to be on the paper." Her excitement grew. "If he's ever been arrested or held down a civil-servant job, or enlisted in the army—"

"His prints would be on file," Tom declared. "Let's go get that form," he proposed eagerly and then paused to suggest a ground rule. "Can we use just one car this time?"

Maintaining her independence took a backseat to

the possibility of a breakthrough. "Sure, why not?" she agreed.

Right now, all that mattered was getting back to the agency before something inadvertently happened to the form the kidnapper had filled out.

"You know," Tom observed as they hurried out of the squad room again, "we don't make such a bad team after all."

The comment made her realize that he'd had the same misgivings about her as she'd had about him when they'd started out.

"No," she allowed, reaching the elevator. "Not so bad." She glanced up on the numbers above the closed stainless-steel doors. Currently, the elevator was on the top floor. "Why don't we use the stairs?"

It wasn't a suggestion. Crossing over to the corner, she was already pulling the door to the stairwell open. He wouldn't have dreamed of attempting to talk her out of it. The police detective from New Mexico was flying on pure adrenaline.

As was he.

Forty-five minutes later, after assuring the uncertain car-rental agency clerk that it was within their authority to commandeer the suspect's application for the van— Tom underscored the fact that a little girl's life was at stake—they obtained the sought-after sheet and slipped it into a clear plastic envelope and quickly returned to the precinct. They went straight down to the lab.

Tom's father was exactly where they had left him, diligently working on the fragments of the dress he'd been brought. Behind him, on the right-hand side of the computer screen, dozens of faces flashed by per minute as the program sought to match the stationary photograph on the left.

"Twice in one day. To what do I owe this second pleasure?" Sean asked, looking up. And then he saw the single sheet of paper Tom held out to him. "Ah, you brought me more. Afraid I'd run out of work?" he asked, amused.

"It's the abductor's application for a rental car," Kait told him. "We're hoping you might be able to lift a clean fingerprint from it."

It wasn't like Tom to miss the bigger picture, Sean thought. Nevertheless, he pointed out the obvious. "The suspect rented a car? Why don't you bring that in? There's bound to be more available prints on it."

The problem there would be in isolating the *right* fingerprints, Sean thought. But nothing was ever easy or cut-and-dried. If it was, it usually turned out to be the wrong answer.

"We would if we could," Kait told him with a frustrated, disappointed sigh. "But nobody's returned the van yet. Something tells me that it probably won't be coming back."

Sean had another opinion. "Don't be so sure."

"Why would he bother?" Kait asked, curious.

"Criminals can surprise you. They have their own strange code to abide by, and while they might kidnap, they won't steal or do something that they think might bring the law down on them more quickly." Having taken the sheet from Tom, Sean carefully removed it from the plastic envelope. "Let me see what I can do with this. Meanwhile—" He nodded toward the computer on his left "—I'm running that photo for you. So far, there's been no match," he said, then smiled for Kait's benefit. "But that doesn't mean there won't be."

"Is he always so optimistic?" she asked Tom as they walked back to the elevator.

Tom laughed softly. "Always. He's very possibly the most upbeat person I've ever known. He always had a way of being able to find a small kernel of good even in the absolutely worst situations."

"The only thing good in this case would be if we do find Megan," Kait said, then grimly tagged on the all-important condition. "Alive."

Tom nodded. A realist, he was still unwilling to even remotely entertain the alternate possibility. But he was aware that even if they did find Megan in time, there might be a wealth of damage to undo. Damage that, most likely, would take long-term counseling before the little girl could even approach normalcy.

"Why don't we see if we can track down that fax number now?"

In her excitement, she'd almost forgotten all about that. Grateful for having something to do, she nodded. "Lead the way. I'm right behind you," she told him.

Yes, Tom thought again, *we really don't make such a bad team after all.*

As it turned out, the fax number didn't belong to a residential home.

They tracked it down to a place of business that handled large volumes of reproductive work for other businesses in the area. Disappointed, they returned to the precinct only to be told by Tom's father that the fingerprints that he managed to lift from the rental application did not match any that could be found in the system.

"So we have a law-abiding abductor who never broke any laws," Kait said in disgust.

"Or, at least, was never caught breaking them," Tom pointed out.

"Well, one way or another, it still doesn't do us any good." She was having a hard time remaining hopeful at this point. "Now what?"

Tom pushed his chair away from his desk and took a deep breath. He knew when to walk away. Not to quit, but to recharge so that he could come at this from a fresh direction. "Now how about I buy you dinner?"

How could he even *think* about eating, she thought, annoyed and edgy. They were running out of time—if they hadn't run out of it already. "I'm not hungry," she told him. "There's got to be something we've missed," she insisted, saying it more to herself than to him.

"And we'll figure it out," he told her, getting up and moving behind her chair, which he pulled away from the desk. "But you haven't eaten anything almost all day, and you can't push yourself like that."

Annoyed, still sitting in the chair, she "walked" herself back in behind the desk. "I've done it before."

"Congratulations." This time, he turned her around in the chair to face him. "But you're not doing it on my watch. Let's go to Malone's."

"What's 'Malone's'?" she asked, still not ready to give in.

"A place where it's too noisy to hear yourself think. Everyone from the precinct turns up there at one time or another to kick back and socialize." He looked at her pointedly. "You could use the break, Kait."

She was about to protest that she was fine, that she didn't need a break and that if he felt he needed one, he was welcome to take it. But while she carried out these arguments in her head, Kait realized that the man was right. She was operating on fumes now and while she wasn't consciously hungry, she did feel pretty wiped out. Maybe if she ate something, she would feel more energetic again.

At the same time, it occurred to her that he'd referred to her by her first name. When had that happened? She wasn't altogether sure if she was comfortable with that. But, like with everything else, she couldn't tell him to stop—because he wouldn't. The man didn't exactly take direction very well.

"Okay, if you're so keen on eating," she said, rising to her feet, "we'll eat."

His grin was just short of triumphant. "Very considerate of you," he said.

She knew the comment was partially sarcastic, but to avoid getting into an argument, she pretended he was serious. "I try," she told him.

Chapter 9

Well, he certainly hadn't exaggerated about the noise, Kait thought half an hour later.

There was a great deal of noise, and it rose and fell like the swell of the tide along the beach. The moment she had opened the door and walked into the publike establishment that, she was told, was like a second home to a great many members of Aurora's police department, the noise had instantly engulfed her.

Seated now at a small table for two with their dinners—cheeseburgers and fries—in front of them, Kait quickly discovered that it was hard to carry on a conversation and even harder to form coherent thoughts and follow them to their logical conclusion. For one thing, she kept getting distracted by a stray fragment of a sentence she'd pick up. For another, people kept stopping by their table for a quick exchange with Tom. She began to think that she was the only one with trouble hearing.

After the last visitor—Dax Cavanaugh, one of the chief of detective's sons—had left once he'd asked them how the investigation was going—he'd met his wife while trying to locate a child who'd been kidnapped from her private school—Kait had turned toward Tom.

"You like this?" she asked, shouting the question at him out of necessity. After half an hour of this, her throat was becoming sore.

In order to hear her better, and to help her hear him, Tom dragged his chair in closer to her until their chairs touched.

"Yeah," he answered, then added with a grin, "I think of it as therapy."

Shaking her head, she looked around at all the people, either seated at the tables or standing lined up along the long bar.

"If you ask me, it's more like being locked up in the insane asylum," she commented.

Since she hadn't shouted the comment, she just assumed he hadn't heard her, which was just as well since it'd been cryptic and somewhat derogatory. But one look at the grin on his face told her that Tom had heard her. How, she had no idea.

"Give yourself time," he counseled. But his words fell on near-deaf ears—and it wasn't by her choice.

Kait shook her head to indicate that she hadn't heard him. "What?"

Leaning in closer still, the side of his arm brushed against hers as he repeated his advice. This time he said it directly into her ear.

Kait heard the words, but that was secondary to the

fact that feeling his warm breath along the side of her face and neck sent one hell of a hot ripple through her body, surging from the point of contact until it touched every part of her and made her far warmer than any heater set on high could have possibly done.

She caught her breath and looked at him, aware that her pulse had accelerated and now went at a rather dangerous, frantic tempo. Even when she'd been threatened with punishment—or worse—as a child, she couldn't remember it ever having reached this wild level.

What was happening here?

He saw the color rising up in her face. Concerned, he asked, "Are you all right?" not realizing that the very act of bringing his lips practically up against her ear was the actual cause of the change in her complexion.

Unsettled, Kait pulled her head back and pressed her lips together. Belatedly, she nodded.

"Yeah. Fine. I'm fine. It's just a little hot in here," she added.

"That's because of all the bodies in here," he guessed. "They generate a lot of heat."

She nodded. It was as good an excuse as any, although he probably didn't believe what he was saying. Not that it wasn't plausible, but the man seemed to have an annoying knack of seeing right into her head, at which point he knew that the temperature of the room had nothing to do with why her own body temperature had gone up.

Still, she went along with what he said, absently raising her shoulders in a careless shrug. "Yeah, that's it, I guess."

"You know," he said after what seemed like a long moment had gone by, "in order for that to do you any good, you actually have to eat it instead of just having it sit on a plate in front of you all evening."

He was referring to her cheeseburger. He'd already finished half of his. The fries that had come with his order were long gone while hers were still sitting on her plate, untouched.

"I don't like wolfing down my food," she answered defensively.

It occurred to her then that the detective with the magnetic blue eyes was watching her lips when she spoke. So that was why he could "hear" her while she was having such trouble hearing him, she thought, annoyed with herself for having missed such a simple explanation.

"I get that," he told her. "But you really should eat it before the turn of the next century."

"Very funny."

In defiance—and to keep from engaging in any more conversation—Kait picked up the cheeseburger and began to eat. It was then when she discovered that, considering it was bar food, the meal in her hands tasted exceptionally good.

Or was she just really hungry?

The latter explanation would mean that Tom was right in his assessment. His penchant for that was getting really annoying, she thought grudgingly.

"Is he driving you crazy yet?"

She heard the question clear as a bell and looked up from her meal to see a petite blonde wearing an unzipped white parka and a tailored, navy blue two-piece suit with a light, pearl-pink shirt peeking out standing beside her.

"Now see what you've done," Tom told his sister

accusingly. "You've made Kaitlyn swallow her tongue instead of her meal."

"I didn't swallow my tongue," Kait protested with feeling, glaring at him. "I was just surprised I could hear her voice so clearly."

Needing no invitation, the other woman pulled over a free chair and turned it around so that it butted up against their tiny table. As she made herself comfortable, her eyes sparkled with a warm greeting.

"Hi, I'm Bridget—one of Thomas's unfortunate sisters," she clarified as an afterthought. "I hear you're Tom's new partner."

"Temporary partner," Kait corrected with more than a little emphasis.

"She's just here until we catch the guy she tracked to our fair city," Tom told his sister. He looked at Bridget pointedly. "Here's a thought. Why don't you pull up a chair and stay awhile?" he suggested, sarcasm masking the deep vein of affection with which he regarded Bridget and all the other members of his immediate family. Unlike some of his friends, he'd never gone through that stage where everyone in his family was both an annoyance and an embarrassment to him.

Bridget's tone was playful. "Thanks, but I can't stay," she said despite the fact that she remained sitting in the chair. "I just wanted to see how our friend from New Mexico was holding up after being subjected to you nonstop." She leaned in closer to Kait's ear. "If you find yourself in need of some embarrassing stories from Thomas's childhood to use as ammunition against him, just let me know." She grinned. "The supply is wide and varied," she promised.

"There aren't any embarrassing stories," Tom said with alacrity. "I was perfect."

Bridget laughed. It was a rich, full-bodied sound that embraced and warmed anyone within earshot. "You keep telling yourself that, big brother," she told Tom. Stealing a French fry off Kait's plate as she rose, Bridget popped it into her mouth, then frowned as it momentarily captured her attention. "These are cold. I'd go and complain if I were you. They'll give you a fresh, warm batch."

"That's Bridget's specialty," he told Kait. "Complaining. She'd complain to God if she got it into her head that he hadn't distributed enough stars in the sky on a particular night."

"Don't listen to a thing he says," Bridget advised the newcomer. "Around the house when we were growing up, we used to call him Pinocchio. He exaggerated and embellished on everything." Her grin widened even though, from where Kait was sitting, that didn't seem possible. Didn't her lips hurt? "See you around, Thomas." And then she winked at Kait just before she left. "Don't let him boss you around. Once he knows he can do that, there's no stopping him."

"Sorry about that," he apologized to Kait once Bridget had woven her way across the floor. The noise swelled again, forcing him to move in even closer to her and repeat what he'd just said.

Kait barely heard him, but it didn't matter. Her mind was otherwise preoccupied. "You're lucky," she said with a touch of wistfulness.

Tom tried to understand why she would say that. "Because I have a sister who likes to embarrass me in front of people?" he asked, bemused.

He wasn't fooling anyone, Kait thought. "I don't think she embarrassed you, and it's obvious that the two of you watch out for each other."

He shrugged carelessly. "In a manner of speaking, I guess," he admitted, then added, "it's a survival tactic. I never know when one of my sisters—or brothers—is going to come swooping in. I definitely never know what's going to come out of their mouths. Watching out for them keeps me on my toes."

Yeah, right. He still wasn't fooling her. While she didn't doubt that he and his siblings probably had their fights, there was no missing the way he felt about them. She would have given anything to have had that kind of an upbringing instead of the one she'd had. Even after Ronald and his wife had adopted her, there were still times when she felt lonely. Back then she would have given anything to have had a sibling, someone she could have shared thoughts and fears with.

"What's it like?" she asked.

"What's what like?"

"Being part of a big family?"

Tom paused and looked around the pub for a moment before answering her question.

"In a way it's kind of like this, I guess. A lot of noise, a lot of pushing and jockeying for position. Wondering if that last piece of pie you've been daydreaming about all through math class will still be there when you get home."

"There was never any pie to wonder about when I was growing up," she told him. "Not until—" Abruptly, Kait stopped talking.

He looked at her, waiting. When she didn't continue, Tom asked, "Until what?"

But Kait just shook her head, more amazed than annoyed. How did this keep happening? "You did it again."

He cocked his head, his eyes on her lips. "Did what again?"

"You got me to talk about myself when I never, ever do that," she insisted.

Tom held his hands up, protesting his innocence. "My hands never left my wrists, so I couldn't have twisted your arm. Every word out of your mouth was voluntary," he concluded. And then his eyes held hers in that way that she found far too intimate to suit her. "Ever think that you secretly *want* to open up about things that happened when you were a kid?"

How she hated being analyzed. "I don't keep secrets from myself."

But he knew better. "Kaitlyn, we *all* keep secrets from ourselves. It helps us maintain a good self-image, which in turn allows us to go on. What are you doing?" he asked abruptly. She'd taken a napkin out of the dispenser and was wrapping up the remainder of her cheeseburger and fries.

"Isn't it obvious?" she challenged through teeth that were all but clenched. "I'm getting this to go."

His own plate was empty and he pushed it aside. "I take it you want to go with it?"

"You take it right." She'd told this man far too much about herself, and it made her feel vulnerable and exposed. Moreover, she had a feeling that this wouldn't be the end of it. And she wasn't thinking just of inadvertently telling him things from her past. The man had a way of getting to her. A way that she was afraid might escalate, and she was no longer as confident that she could keep him at arm's length if that happened.

Her reaction to him just now, when she'd felt his breath along her skin, had been too intense. It was a matter of better safe than sorry.

"Look, maybe I'd better get a hotel room for the duration that I'm out here—" she began to propose.

"We can talk about that when we get home," Tom promised.

He was just humoring her, she thought. And anyway, what was there to "talk" about? The decision, one way or another, was hers to make. Hers alone.

She debated digging in, but the truth of the matter was that she still felt pretty tired and the prospect of having to trudge to some hotel—after she actually located an acceptable one—was not exactly something she looked forward to.

Okay, tomorrow, she promised herself. Tomorrow she'd find a hotel and check in. For now she supposed she could put up with being around the cocky detective with the bedroom eyes for one more night.

She *could* resist him for one more night. It was an order.

Absorbed in thought, Kait didn't see the tall, handsome silver-haired man until she'd all but walked on top of him.

Startled, she immediately took a step back, an apology instantly rising to her lips. "I'm sorry, I wasn't paying attention where I was—"

She got no further. The stranger was smiling at her. The smile, she realized with a jolt, was reminiscent of the one she used to see on Ronald's lips. It had the same kind of kindly understanding behind it.

It brought back memories. And instantly softened her toward this stranger whose foot she realized she'd stepped on.

"I'm sure you didn't. The fault's all mine," Andrew Cavanaugh told her, absolving her of any blame. "I was so intent on getting to Tom here before the two of you left that I just got in your way."

"You were looking for me, Chief?" Tom asked, surprised. While Malone's was a favorite hangout for the police department, the former chief of police didn't come by very often. He preferred having the men on the force drop by his home where he could feed them while they visited. His meals, as well as his parties, were legendary.

"Please," Andrew protested, "I haven't been 'Chief' in a hundred years." Or so it felt, anyway, although he had always been the first to maintain that while you could take the cop out of the uniform, you couldn't take the uniform out of the cop. "Just call me Uncle Andrew," he urged. "Or, if that feels too heavy for your tongue," he added in an understanding tone, "just Andrew will be fine with me."

The man would never be "just Andrew," and they both knew it, Tom thought. There was a quality about this man that made you instantly sit up and take notice of him whenever he entered a room. It was the kind of quality found in all the leaders beloved by their men, leaders whose men would follow them through the gates of hell just because they were at the front of the column.

"'Uncle is going to take a little time," Tom admitted honestly.

The tall man inclined his head. "Andrew, then," Andrew agreed.

Had they casually met at the bar and he had had no knowledge about the man, Tom wouldn't have had any trouble referring to him by just his first name. But knowing that Andrew Cavanaugh had once been a highly respected chief of police, as well as being the patriarch of a large, sprawling family, not to mention this latest twist which had brought to light that he was also his uncle, made referring to him by his first name utterly impossible for him.

So Tom compromised. "How about if I just call you 'sir' until the uncle part gets comfortable?"

"'Sir' it is," Andrew said with a laugh.

And then he shifted his deep blue eyes to Kait. "I'm Andrew Cavanaugh," he told her, extending his hand to the young woman. "The former chief of police," he added.

"Detective Kaitlyn Two Feathers," she told him, taking the offered hand and shaking it. "Nice to meet you, sir."

As before, his smile encompassed her. "Nice to meet you, too. And I already know who you are."

"He knows everything," a young woman who bore more than a passing resemblance to Tom's sister Bridget informed her, coming up behind them.

Another one of his sisters? Kait wondered.

"Don't even think you have a prayer of keeping anything from him. We all made that mistake when we were growing up. And we all got caught," she added with a sigh. Rising up on her toes, she brushed a kiss against Andrew's cheek. "Hi, Dad."

He kissed her back, then laughed. "As always, you're

exaggerating, Rayne," Andrew told his youngest. Affection throbbed in every syllable. Looking at Kait, he assured her, repeating, "She's exaggerating. As the baby of the family, she tended to do that a lot because we indulged her."

"No more than he did anyone else in the family," Rayne confided to Kait.

"I'll be out of your way in a second," Andrew promised his new nephew and the young woman with him.

"I just wanted to invite you over to the house tomorrow. I'm having a get-together at five o'clock. Your father's already coming and so are your sisters and brothers, and I'd appreciate seeing you there, as well."

It wasn't an invitation so much as a command performance, Tom thought, amused. "Uncle" or "Chief," you just didn't say no to the man. There was just no way.

"You, too, Detective," Andrew told Kait, catching her off guard. "You're more than welcome to come. The more, the merrier."

"And he won't take no for an answer," Rayne added, "so don't even bother making excuses. He won't accept them."

"This time, she's not exaggerating," Andrew told the duo, though he seemed to be addressing Kait more than his nephew. "I'll look forward to seeing the two of you there," he promised just before he slipped away to deliver other invitations.

Stunned like someone who had just been blitzkrieged, Kait hardly remembered going out the door and leaving Malone's behind.

Were all the Cavanaughs trained in disarming the world at-large?

Chapter 10

It occurred to Kait belatedly what had been nagging at her as she'd spoken to the former chief of police. He looked like Tom's father. If not for what might have been a height difference, they could have been identical twins. In a town as small as hers, the similarity would have been noticed instantly, not over five decades later.

But there were differences, she thought as she sat in the passenger seat of Tom's car. Tom's father, while certainly no shrinking violet, was less dynamic than Andrew Cavanaugh. The latter had instantly commandeered the immediate area just by his appearance alone.

"He just materializes out of thin air and tells you to come over for a command performance?"

Although they hadn't exchanged any words since they'd left Malone's, Tom knew immediately that she was referring to the former chief.

"Pretty much."

She looked at Tom's profile. He didn't strike her as someone who could be ordered around, no matter how sugarcoated that command might sound when it was issued. "And you go?"

He heard the challenge in her voice and laughed softly. Not everything was meant to be a battle. He wondered if she would ever take that to heart.

"The man knows how to do things with food that you can't begin to imagine. It borders on the magical," he told her.

"So you go because you like to eat?"

There was a sarcastic note in Kait's voice, but he could tell she didn't believe the excuse he'd just uttered for a minute. Which meant, at bottom, that she gave him credit for not being shallow—whether she knew it or not.

"I go because I like keeping an open mind. This, as it turns out, is my father's family and so, now it's mine, as well. Up until a few months ago, I knew them as 'the Cavanaughs,' good people, great cops. It's interesting getting to know them on a more personal level, as my cousins, uncles and aunts." He glanced in her direction. "In my position, you wouldn't?"

Her shoulders stiffened in a defensive move he was becoming pretty familiar with. "We're not talking about me, we're talking about you."

Tom deliberately kept his tone mild, upbeat. "Gee, I thought we were just talking in general." And then he grew a little more serious. "I'm not asking probing questions, Kait. I'm just asking general questions. It's called conversation. What are you afraid I might find out about you?"

"I am not afraid," she said sharply. "I am *never* afraid."

"Okay." He stretched out the word as if it had twice as many syllables. "So, you think the sun's going to rise again tomorrow?"

She stared at him. "What?"

"I'm looking for nice, safe topics that don't rub you the wrong way. I figure it's okay to talk about the sun. It can be the moon if you'd rather talk about that." He gestured toward the hills in the background as he drove by them. "Or coyotes." A few of the creatures had been known to turn up in the residential area on occasion, foraging for food.

The absurdity of what he had just said made Kait laugh. And relent.

"Okay," she conceded. "Maybe I'm being a little up-tight."

"Nah," Tom dismissed.

She continued as if he hadn't said anything. "It's just that I'm not used to having to make any conversation at all. Like I told you when we first started, I don't usu-ally work with a partner."

"Maybe you should. They say that a little verbal give-and-take is healthy for you. Keeps you on your toes, keeps your brain thinking and the juices flowing."

She took the last part of what he said to be criticism of her lone-wolf approach to her work. "My juices are flowing just fine, thank you."

He spared her a long glance as they stood idling at a red light. The corners of his mouth curved. "Won't get an argument out of me."

Why that comment, as well as the sensual look in his eyes, would cause a flash of warmth to pass over her, she couldn't—or wouldn't—answer. But there was no denying that she felt warmer. So much so that she un-buttoned her jacket.

"By the way," he continued as they drove the last leg of the trip, "the chief was serious when he extended that invitation to you to come to his party."

She was about to shrug it off, then realized what Tom was saying to her by repeating the former police chief's impromptu invitation. "Do you want me to go with you?"

Put that way, he knew she'd turn it down. "You make it sound as if I want you to hold my hand at the get-together. What I want—and what the chief wants—is for you to go for you," he told her. "Like I said, I think it might do you some good to get out and socialize. And if nothing else, the Cavanaughs know how to have a good time."

This was uncharted territory for her. It had to stop here, before it was too late. Before she was no longer in control of the situation—the way she was afraid might happen.

"Look, let's get something straight. I came here to keep a promise. I want to find a little girl and catch a predator. I didn't come out here looking to fill my dance card."

Tom nodded, humoring her. "Dancing isn't required. Just as long as you show up at his party."

Okay, this really had gone too far. She looked at Tom incredulously. "Because if I don't, what? He'll miss me?" she asked sarcastically. "Hell, the man won't even know I'm not there."

Now there she was wrong. "Trust me, from what I've heard about Andrew Cavanaugh, he'll know. Not only that, but it's highly likely he might turn up at your doorstep the next day, asking why you decided not to come."

"It's your doorstep," she pointed out stubbornly, clinging to semantics.

He didn't bother pointing out that she was nitpicking. "Makes it that much worse."

Her eyes narrowed. "And how is that?" she asked.

Without her realizing it, they'd arrived at the house.

Tom stopped the car, parking it in the driveway beside hers. The contrast was hard to miss. Her vehicle was over ten years old and still bore the dust of the highways between New Mexico and Northern California that she'd taken to get here. His vehicle was close to pristine.

Unbuckling his seat belt, he looked at her. "It means I'm responsible for you in a way and I should have found a way to get you to come."

Okay, now that had gone over the edge. After getting out of the car, Kait slammed the door on her side. Hard. Frustrated by her inability to make headway in the abduction case, she needed an object to take it out on. His words had waved a red flag right in front of her.

"No one's responsible for me," she ground out between clenched teeth. "And that includes you, so if you know what's good for you, Detective, you'll get that through your head."

If she was hoping to bait him and draw him into an argument, he would disappoint her. Once out of the vehicle, he locked it automatically as he asked, "Don't you ever get lonely in that world you've barricaded yourself inside of?"

She'd watched him disarm the security system once

and had retained the sequence he'd used. She used it now and stormed into the house ahead of him. The moment he followed, she whirled around, her eyes flashing.

"Stop trying to analyze me!" she shouted. "Just leave me alone!"

And that, too, was another part of the problem, he thought. "I think you've been left alone too much," he countered.

She threw up her hands. "I don't care what you think!" Sucking in a breath to steady herself, she found it wasn't working. Neither was staying under the same roof with this man who made her feel so tense, so edgy. And so very, very angry beyond all reason. "This was a dumb idea," she announced. With that, she headed back for the front door.

Anticipating what she'd do next, Tom moved fast and reached the door before she did. He placed himself in front of it.

"Where are you going?" he asked.

"Where I should have gone the first night I got to Aurora. To find a hotel. Thank you for your hospitality," she retorted grudgingly as an afterthought. "Now get the hell out of my way."

He stood his ground and continued to block the door. "I don't want you out on the road like this."

"You don't seem to understand you don't have a say in this. You don't have a say in any of it!" Kait shouted.

She stuck her chin out, daring him to contradict her. Her eyes were blazing and she was breathing hard, as if she'd just run a record-breaking mile instead of just moving a few feet. Furious when he wouldn't step aside,

Kait grabbed him by his arms, intending to physically shove him aside.

That was the last thing she remembered clearly because instead of shoving him, she found herself somehow entangled with him. His hands were on her waist and somewhere in the back of her head. She knew he meant to hold her in place, to stop her from leaving.

What it all boiled down to be was the classic case of the immovable object meeting the irresistible force. She didn't know which of them was which. All she knew was that she didn't wind up shoving him aside and he didn't quite succeed in holding her in place.

What happened was, like similar poles of a magnet, they were suddenly, inexplicably, pulled together, her body fitting up against his as if they were actually two halves of the same whole.

The moment they came together, the heat sizzled through her, setting every inch of her body, inside and out, on fire.

Stunned, Kait stared up at him, words evaporating from not just her lips but from her brain, as well. The look in his eyes told her that he was pretty much experiencing the same thing.

Either that, or he knew how to mimic the reaction to perfection.

The very next instant, it no longer mattered if she could talk or think clearly enough to form words. Because she wouldn't have been able to say any of them.

Her mouth was pressed urgently against his.

Whether she had moved to kiss him, or he had moved to kiss her, was unknown and completely irrelevant. What *was* relevant was that they were sealed within this kiss, standing in an inferno that gave every indication of burning them both up to a crisp before the night got too much older.

She'd been angry before, hurt before, lost before. But she had never, *ever* felt like this before, never reacted like this before. Any other time, with any other man, she would have shoved him away, sending him sprawling after separating the two of them with a well-aimed, painful thrust to his manhood with her knee.

But the truth of it was—a truth that shook her down to her very core—that she didn't *want* to be separated from him. Didn't want him to draw his lips—or his body—away from hers.

She wanted to kiss him and *be* kissed by him.

And more than that.

She desperately wanted more than that.

She still wasn't thinking, wasn't upbraiding herself or even wondering what the hell had come over her. She was just acting—and reacting. Because while the kiss deepened to the point that it had utterly swallowed her up, sending her into a world where nothing else existed outside of the fiery pit she was standing in, she was vaguely aware that her hands, acting independently of any actual thought process, were all but ripping the clothes right off Tom's body.

And he was doing the same to her.

Except he was more gentle about it, not ripping anything but tugging it away, sliding it off, opening buttons, slipping down zippers.

And touching.

Touching her flesh, exploring her body, curving his fingertips along her skin as if she was a book written in braille and he was just learning how to read.

Excitement pulsed through her.

Every pass of his hand increased the fire in her veins. She had passed the point of sanity and was now, she knew, genuinely certifiable.

There was no other explanation for why she was reacting this way, why this incredibly intense hunger had risen within her out of nowhere. And now this same hunger was bent on consuming him, on having him take her and thus creating, she knew with confidence, that earthquake within her that promised to completely rock the foundations of her world.

Tom had no idea what had come over him.

One minute all he was trying to do was to keep her from running off into the night half-cocked, a car accident looking to happen, and the next minute...

The next minute he found himself acting out the fantasy that had been echoing in his brain from the first moment he laid eyes on the redhead with the improbable name and the killer curves.

But, attracted or not—and he was, to a degree that utterly defied description—he'd never behaved like a knuckle-dragging caveman with any woman. He'd been raised to respect women, to watch carefully for signals that told him whether or not there was any interest in a fleeting meeting of the minds and bodies. When there was—when it was mutual—there was no question that it was always enjoyable.

But one thing never changed. He had always been in control, always been able to think coherently. He'd never felt anything that had driven him to the brink of mindlessness—and beyond.

That one thing that never changed had changed now. All of this was happening in a steam roomlike haze. Any thoughts he had were scrambled and reduced to single words, as if he was a toddler just learning his way around voicing his feelings.

Except that nothing in his vocabulary could begin to describe or express what was going on inside him right then. He hadn't the words for it because he'd never had this feeling before. He was vaguely aware that he should step back, should ask her if she was all right with this, but he couldn't. Couldn't ask, couldn't speak.

Couldn't stop.

He wanted to pleasure her, make certain that she received as well as gave, but she sapped away all of his energy, reducing him to a palpitating mass of jelly.

The hot, erotic dance that had sprung up so spontaneously culminated in his joining together with her, filling her in fact much the way she filled him in spirit.

They were both scrambling up the side of the volcano, bent on reaching the top before it was too late.

And then it was happening.

The eruption came, sending him hurdling toward the sky. From the way she'd cried out as she arched beneath him, her fingertips digging into his back, he knew that he'd taken her with him.

Satisfaction spread out like sunbeams inside him and he did his best to hold on to them just as he held on to her, pulling Kait tightly against him.

He could feel her heart pounding against his until the rhythm became one.

Just as they had become one.

The scent of her hair filled his head, and he clung to it.

Just as he continued to hold on as tightly as he could to the sensation—and to her—for as long as he could, loath to let either go even though he knew that he'd have to.

Eventually.

But not yet.

Not yet.

Chapter 11

"Are you all right?"

She was lying on the oversize sofa, naked, next to a man she'd known for only a few days. There was no graceful way out of this, Kait thought. For now, she didn't upbraid herself for getting into this position in the first place. That would come later, after she was dressed and somewhere else.

The only thing she could do now was reach for her customary blasé attitude and cloak herself in it as best she could. "Is that your way of asking, 'How was I?'?"

Tom shifted a fraction of an inch so that he could prop himself up on his elbow and look at her. Given the lack of space and that he was on the outside, barely balancing his body on the sofa's edge, it was a tricky maneuver, but he managed.

"No, that's my way of asking if you're all right."

He searched her face for any telltale signs that would answer his question, since he was fairly certain that she wouldn't. "I didn't hurt you, did I?"

Defensive, flippant words all crowded on her lips, ready for release. But she didn't find what she expected in Tom's eyes or in his expression. He didn't look cocky or full of himself. Instead, he seemed genuinely concerned.

Maybe she'd been wrong about him. Maybe he wasn't like all the others.

Yeah, and maybe pigs really do fly when you're not looking.

"Why would you think you hurt me?" she challenged, raising her chin.

The chip on her shoulder was back, Tom thought. But now he didn't just suspect, he *knew* that there was a different woman beneath all that bravado and that leading-with-her-chin anger. The woman he'd made love with was soft, vulnerable and, unless he'd misread the signs, in desperate need of love.

"Because I went at it a little aggressively and a little too fast," he replied.

Did the man have amnesia? They *both* went at it that way. If anything, she'd been even more aggressive than he'd been because her clothes weren't torn from her body the way she had torn his clothes away from his. Her sudden, intense eagerness to make love with him had eaten up her common sense and control.

"I'm not complaining," she retorted, then pointedly asked, "are you?"

Tom looked at her as if she just wasn't making any sense. "Why would I complain about being allowed a quick jaunt through the gates of paradise?"

She wouldn't have thought that he was the type who could lay it on. "Paradise, huh? And the earth moved for you, did it?" she asked, upset that he was making fun of her.

She wanted to bait him, to pick a fight again, Tom thought. Why couldn't she just accept things at face value once in a while? Why couldn't she enjoy them? Just how destructive had those years in foster care been for her? He had to bite his tongue to keep from asking.

"The earth, the sky, the sea, take your pick. None of it remained stationary."

"That good, huh?" This time, he noticed, the edgy, sarcastic challenge was, for the most part, gone from her voice.

He watched her, wanting to take her back into his arms, wanting desperately to revisit the mind-blowing terrain they had just covered. But he knew that this time he would have to go slower. And, he had to get her to trust him for more than a couple of moments.

His voice low, serious, he answered her question by echoing her words back to her. "That good."

What kind of power did this man have over her? She knew he was just making it all up, feeding her lines so that maybe he could get in a second quickie before he went off to his room.

And yet…

And yet she wanted to believe him. More than that, his words aroused her, made her not just want to believe him but made her want him, as well. The heat, the desire, the fire, they were all back. And he hadn't even so much as touched her again.

At least, not physically. Emotionally was a whole other story.

"You're cold," he noted.

There were goose bumps on her arms, she realized, but it wasn't the cold that had caused them.

She didn't want to come across as the eager one, not again, so she murmured in agreement, "Maybe just a little."

What happened next caught them both off guard. He reached for the colorful throw that had fallen off the sofa when they had engaged one another in that race to the top of the summit. But as he stretched out his arm for it, the movement threw him off balance and off his precarious perch on the sofa, as well.

Tom started to fall and reacted automatically without thinking. He made a grab for something. That something turned out to be Kait. And suddenly, they were both falling.

He landed on the floor with the rug at his back and Kait at his front. Twisting, she had managed to land right on top of him, her body sealed to his in a close approximation of the erotic dance that had just transpired minutes ago.

"Sorry," he apologized, stifling the laugh that bubbled up in his throat. "I wanted to grab something to make you warmer."

He watched in fascination as a smile blossomed on her lips and spread to her eyes. She'd never smiled with her eyes before. It made her even more beautiful.

"And you thought you'd accomplish that by grabbing me?" she asked, amused, though she was trying hard not to be.

"That was an accident," he told her honestly. "I was trying to reach the blanket for you."

Why did something so simple mean so much to her?

It wasn't as if he had to outrun a cheetah to get it for her. And yet, his thoughtfulness got to her. And definitely raised his stock in her eyes by two hundred percent.

"Well, now that we're here like this," she proposed. "We might as well make the best of it."

The grin on his lips went straight to her heart, as well as parts beyond. She was now definitely warmer. "I thought we already were," he said to her softly, moving just enough to establish his point.

"So we are," she agreed.

He framed her face between his hands and brought her mouth down to his. And those gates he'd mentioned earlier, the ones that led straight to paradise, opened up right before her startled eyes.

And invited her in.

Kait didn't really remember what came next, or in what order. Only that she enjoyed it. Every second of it. Immensely.

She didn't recall falling asleep, either. But she must have because she was opening her eyes now and in order to do that, at some point they must have closed.

Closed tightly, she deduced, because she wasn't on the living-room sofa anymore, or even the floor next to it. She was in a warm bed. Not the one she'd been frequenting these past few nights, but a wider one.

And, now that she focused, it was definitely a masculine one.

The bed was a four-poster that looked as if it had been fashioned in the middle of some forest and shipped out the second the trees had been felled and sections had been carved out to form this massive, dark piece of furniture. The bureau could be described the same way, as could the nightstand. All made with wood as dark as midnight.

Above her, decorative beams were built into the cathedral ceiling. Definitely a place where Grizzly Adams would have felt right at home. Except the man with whom she'd made love with not once or twice but—if memory served—a total of three times last night was as removed from the persona of someone typified by the label "Grizzly" as the earth was from the moon. Tom had been gentle and surprisingly tender. More so each time they did it.

The woman who finally landed him was going to be very, very lucky, Kait couldn't help thinking.

"'Morning, Detective Two Feathers," he whispered against her ear softly.

Whispered or not, she jumped as if he'd just leaped out from behind a building and yelled out "Boo." For a second, her heart almost leaped out of her chest.

"I thought you were asleep," she told him.

The grin he sported encompassed his entire face. "Nope," he told her. "I woke up a little more than half an hour ago."

And he had just stayed in bed? Tom didn't strike her as the type who was lazy and content just to while away the time in bed. He was a doer. Or had she been wrong about that?

"Why didn't you get up?"

He pretended to be surprised at the suggestion. "And what? Miss the show?"

Puzzled, she looked at him. She hadn't a clue what he was talking about. "What show?"

The grin grew softer, almost sentimental. That also

didn't fit in with the personality she'd attributed to him so far.

"The one right in front of me," he told her. "I've been watching you sleep. You're a lot more expressive when you sleep. You even smile sometimes. You looked almost soft that way. Made me want to ask you what you were smiling about. Except in order to do that, I'd have to wake you up, and I really didn't want to disturb you."

He couldn't be that thoughtful—or could he?

Kait shook her head. "I can't figure out if you're really on the level, Cavanaugh, or if you're making fun of me."

So they were back to last names, were they? Did that mean that the party was over? The thought brought a pang to him. "Why would I make fun of you, Detective Two Feathers?"

That sounded way too formal, even if he was just kidding. "You've seen me naked, so I think you can keep calling me by my first name," she told him.

Tom mulled over her words, pretending to be intrigued. "Is that your criteria for informality? Someone has to see you naked?"

She blew out an impatient breath. "Do you ever stop asking questions?" she wanted to know.

He thought for a moment, then shook his head. "Not often. It's what makes me a good detective," he said with all sincerity. And then a glint of mischief entered his eyes. "But there is one surefire way to stop me from asking questions," he told her. Shifting so that he could easily trace the curve of her cheek with his fingertips— which he did slowly—he smiled into her eyes. "Guess what it is?"

Kait laughed, a trace of nervousness bubbling up in her throat—why, she couldn't begin to guess. "More questions."

She was about to show him rather than just make a verbal "guess," but just as she raised her head to kiss him, the phone on the nightstand rang. The jarring, insistent noise broke the spell the moment had woven around them.

"You better answer it," she told him, sitting up.

She drew the blanket around her, thinking that the bedroom felt a little chilly now that her body was separated from his by this distance. Kait tried to remember just where her clothes were. She began to get up and suddenly sucked in her breath as Tom snaked his arm around her waist.

The smile on his lips, even as he was talking to someone on the phone, was meant just for her. He kept his arm where it was, intent on preventing her from getting up. She heard him agreeing with someone on the other end of the line, promising solemnly to be "there," wherever "there" was.

"Another crime scene?" she asked.

It was Saturday, but there was no such thing as a day off if you worked for the police department. If there was a crime and your name was up in the rotation, you had to come down, even during Christmas dinner.

Not that that had been a problem of hers for the past four years. Dinner on Christmas was just like dinner any other day for her. It amounted to something that came either directly out of the freezer in her refrigerator or from a takeout place between the precinct and her apartment. Nothing fancy, just a snack to sustain her until the next meal, whenever that might come up.

Tom laughed. "Only if we don't show up," he told her. When she looked at him quizzically, he said, "That was Andrew Cavanaugh, making sure you and I were coming to the get-together today. He thought the invitation might have slipped our minds."

The former chief had extended the invitation only last night. "Why would he think that?"

Tom looked at her knowingly. The woman was the antithesis of a social butterfly. "He's a good judge of character, I hear."

That was debatable, she thought, but she wasn't going to get sucked into a debate she probably didn't have a prayer of winning. So she asked the question that had been nagging at her mind.

"Why is it so important to Cavanaugh that we show up?"

That went hand in hand with the way the man felt about family. Tom tried to put it succinctly for her. "The way I hear it, family's the most important thing in the world to the man. To all of the Cavanaughs," he added.

She supposed there had to be more than one man like that. After all, Ronald had been like that. He'd been the only family she'd really known—and that had been completely of his choosing. He could have walked away when he turned her over to social services—but he didn't. He kept on coming back until he could finally take her into his own home, first as a foster child and then as his own adopted daughter.

"Okay, I'll buy that," she conceded. "But I'm not family."

There Tom had to contradict her. "It's not always blood that makes a family," Tom told her. As he talked, he paused to combine his words with gestures, lightly passing his lips along the slopes of her shoulders. "To Andrew Cavanaugh, every good cop is part of his extended family."

"You realize you're making it very hard for me to think when you're doing that," she told him, grabbing his hand as he trailed his fingertips between her breasts.

But she couldn't quite make herself push him away.

"I'm counting on that," he teased. He pressed a kiss to the dip of her collarbone and then progressed down farther to where his fingers had last lingered.

She struggled to focus her mind, which began to drift again. "You can't tell me that you're ready to do it again," she said in disbelief.

"I wasn't planning on telling you. I was planning on showing you," he said quietly after a beat. "I initially set out on a very noble mission," he informed her with almost a completely straight face.

Lord, but he was doing wonderfully arousing things to her, wreaking havoc on her thought process.

"And that was?" she asked with effort.

"I wanted to help you unwind. You were much too tense." And then he grinned. "Mission is almost accomplished. You're almost unwound. A couple more times should do it."

"A couple more..." She blinked in disbelief. "Are you a man or a machine?"

"I guess we're about to find out," Tom theorized. He moved his lips up along her throat slowly until they reached hers.

The rest of the discussion was tabled. Indefinitely.

* * *

"You came!" Andrew declared with palatable pleasure late that afternoon. He had thrown open the door the moment Tom had rung the bell.

The only way the man could have anticipated his arrival, Tom thought, was if he had a surveillance monitor mounted somewhere on the other side of the door to go with what he assumed was a hidden camera on the outside of the entrance.

"It was a royal invitation," Kait answered before Tom had an opportunity to reply. "To refuse seemed treasonous."

Rather than issue a disclaimer, or frown sternly at the remark, Andrew turned his attention momentarily toward his new nephew and laughed heartily.

"This one catches on fast."

And then suddenly Andrew turned his full attention on her. The smile he flashed at her stripped Kait of any residual suspicions or leery feelings she might have toward him or the whole gathering in general. It somehow managed to scoop her up out of the realm of "outsider" and made her one of them.

"I'm very glad you decided to humor me and come with Tom, Kaitlyn. I'll try very hard to make sure you won't regret your decision." He turned toward Tom. "Your father's already here. He, Kendra and Bridget are out on the patio, talking with Brian. He's more or less the family historian," he said, confiding in Tom. "Your dad's full of questions, as any of us would be, given the circumstances."

He guided them both through the foyer and then pointed to what looked like a family room tucked away at the rear of the house. Blocking part of the view was the biggest Christmas tree she had ever seen. It looked to be about ten feet tall and absolutely laden with decorations. Left on her own, she would have been satisfied to stare at it all day.

"The patio's just beyond that," Andrew was telling them. "If either one of you find yourself needing anything, just give a yell. I'll hear you eventually," he promised. "In the meantime, feel free to dig in. The table's still full but there's plenty more if that runs out. Never sent anyone home hungry yet," he told them with a wink. "By the way, Kait, you might enjoy meeting Brian's stepson's wife. Her name was Julianne White Bear before she crossed paths with Frank. Like you, she came here following up leads in a case that started out in her home state." Andrew smiled. "After she accomplished what she set out to do, she decided that maybe Aurora had a few things to offer that she couldn't find back in Arizona."

To be polite, Kait asked, "And what was it that she couldn't find in Arizona?"

The wide, pleased, not to mention radiant smile was back. "Frank."

The next moment, Andrew had melded into the crowd, responding to someone who had called out to him. For the first time, Kait was able to focus on the number of people who literally filled the house to overflowing. She turned to Tom with wonder in her eyes. "Are all these people actually—"

"Cavanaughs?" he ended her sentence for her. "One way or the other, mostly, yes."

"What do you mean one way or another?"

"Well, if I have my figures correct, Andrew has five kids—all married with families of their own. Brian had four with his first wife. When she died, he eventually married his old partner, who has four of her own." He paused and laughed at the confusion on Kait's face. "Are you keeping up on this?"

"Just barely," she admitted.

"That gives Brian four kids and four stepkids—"

"And they're all married?" she asked.

"Yup. Then there's the group that belongs to Mike—"

She cocked her head, as if the information made it list to one side. "And that is…?"

"Was," Tom corrected. "Andrew and Brian's brother who died in the line of duty. He had two kids with his wife and apparently three more with a mistress. I hear they're all married, too. And then there's us," he concluded. "My siblings and me," he clarified in case she thought he was referring to himself and her.

"You people should issue scorecards at the door," she told him.

"I hear that they're seriously thinking about it," he answered with a laugh. Taking her arm, he coaxed her to come along. "Let's go talk to my dad and see if he's as overwhelmed as you are."

She would have argued with him—she didn't like being perceived as out of her depth—but in this case, it was really true.

Chapter 12

"So what do you think of them?" Tom asked her as they drove home much later that evening.

As the day had worn on, Kait had found herself drawn into discussions where her opinion was genuinely sought. The Cavanaughs wouldn't allow her to sit silently on the sidelines, much as she would have wanted to.

The one thing that *all* the Cavanaughs seemed to have in common was that participation was encouraged and actively urged.

"They all seemed very nice," Kait granted, then couldn't help adding, "I also think there were probably less people in my dad's tribe than I saw at that house today."

Tom slanted a look in her direction. She'd opened

the door and he took the advantage to slip in. "I've been meaning to ask you about that."

She wasn't aware that she'd said anything that begged for an answer. "About what?"

"Your last name."

That again. "What about it?" Kait asked, instantly on her guard.

Just because she'd been sucked into one conversation after another when they'd been at the former chief of police's house didn't mean she wanted to bare her own soul.

Tom began slowly, like someone trying to gain the confidence of a skittish colt that hadn't been tamed yet. "You're a redhead."

There was no denying that, so she just moved on. "Yes?"

"A real redhead," he emphasized. She had that true, warm reddish hue that no bottle of hair dye could begin to approximate. "I've never seen a Native American of *any* tribe with red hair."

That was because she wasn't a Navajo. She was Irish and Welsh with some other parts she had no direct knowledge of thrown into the mix, as well.

"Maybe you've been sheltered," she answered loftily. "I can't help it if you don't get out much."

He'd thought that interacting with the Cavanaughs would get her to open up a little, but he'd obviously underestimated her stubbornness.

He sighed. "You're still not going to tell me, are you?"

She laughed quietly, pleased that he seemed resigned that she wouldn't tell him anything. "A little bit of mystery is good. Keeps things lively."

He thought of last night. They'd come close to setting the bedsheets on fire. "I don't think there were any complaints in that department. At least I know I don't have any." He glanced at Kait again as a streetlight they drove past lit up the car's interior. "Do you?"

"Complaints?"

This was the part where she made a comment so blasé that he wouldn't know or even guess just how much she'd enjoyed last night. How much his lovemaking had pleasured her down to the very core.

But when she opened her mouth, her lips betrayed her—much the way they had last night, when she was the one who essentially began the torrid night of lovemaking.

"No, none."

He knew to grin outright would most likely cost him his head—or some other, possibly more vital part of him—so he suppressed any outward signs of victory as best he could.

"As a matter of fact," he said with growing enthusiasm, "I have nothing but high marks, praise and commendations to give you."

He ended the sentence on a high note, as if he expected her to come in and add her two cents, Kait thought. She merely smiled at him and said, "Don't push it, Detective."

Arriving at the house, Tom pulled his vehicle into the driveway and turned off the ignition. But rather than get out, he turned and faced her. "You're being formal again."

She felt as if she was struggling to keep even a semblance of a wall up. Her need to protect herself was great, but she was having a great deal of trouble executing the necessary steps for that to continue. He'd managed to all but burn away her defenses.

"Shouldn't I be?" she asked, struggling to sound distant.

"You can if you want to," he allowed. "Makes it a little strange kissing you, but I'll manage."

She would have been lying if she didn't admit, at least to herself, that tonight had been in the back of her mind the entire day. Specifically, what it would be like once they were back at his house with the party behind them and the prospect of lovemaking tantalizingly shimmering before them. Would he want a repeat of last night, or was he one of those men who lost interest after the conquest had taken place and the challenge was no longer there?

But now that he'd said what he had about kissing her, she felt that at least tonight would be wonderful. Tonight they'd make love again.

The idea pleased her more than she was happy about. Because she didn't want to count on anything outside of herself, and this was definitely counting on him.

"So you plan on kissing me." It wasn't so much a question as an establishment of fact.

"As long as you don't have any objections," Tom told her. "If you don't, I plan to kiss you until both of us are returned to our ancient liquid states."

They each got out of the car and walked up to the front door. Tom did the honors, temporarily disarming the security system so that he could open the door for them. All the while, he continued to look at her.

"Doesn't sound like much of a plan," she told him loftily as she walked in. "Actually, it sounds like the waste of an evening."

Shutting the door behind them, Tom caught her lightly by the arm. When she looked up at him, he smiled into her eyes. "The plan doesn't end there."

"Oh?" Damn, she had to keep her heart from kicking into high gear like that. She would wind up giving herself away—if she hadn't already. "Go on."

"I have an idea," he proposed, slipping her jacket off her shoulders and down her arms. He tossed the jacket in the general direction of the easy chair. "Instead of telling you, why don't I show you?" His smile widened. "I tend to be a hands-on kind of guy."

"Sounds interesting," she agreed.

The next moment, he surprised her by pushing her back. She felt her back meeting the wall in the living room. In the next breath, the front of her body was securely lodged against his. So much so that their complementing body parts meshed in a whispered promise of things to come.

If she had any illusions about remaining aloof or projecting an aura of disinterest, they all went up in smoke the first few seconds into the seduction. Her pulse raced in tandem with her heart rate and all she could think of was Tom. The way he made her feel, the way she wanted to make *him* feel.

They went as fast, if not faster, as they had the very first time they'd made love last night. There was an urgency, fueled by a fear that something would happen to terminate all this, and she desperately wanted to experience that light show in the sky that Tom could create within her just as they reached the ultimate climax together.

She wasn't disappointed.

When it happened, when the stars seemed to shower

down all around them, Kait could feel his heart slamming against hers even as he continued to balance the weight of his body on his elbows, keeping it from crushing her.

As the euphoria began to recede, she heard Tom laugh very softly to himself. Her insecurity instantly perceived it to reflect something she had done that he found laughable.

Stiffening, she challenged, "What?"

He'd had every intention of going slow, but she'd tempted him into a faster and faster tempo. He didn't like to admit it to himself, but she had wrested control away from him. He couldn't remember that ever happening before.

"We went at it like the end of the world was around the corner."

Was he going to say it hadn't been any good that fast? Because he had rocked her world, just as he had yesterday. But maybe today he'd been removed enough to feel the need to criticize her.

"So?" she asked defensively.

"So this time," he said, gently gliding the crook of his finger along her cheek, "I'd like to do it as if we had all the time in the world."

Her eyes widened as a pleased feeling spread all through her. "You want to do it again?"

He mimicked her surprise. "You don't?"

She blew out a breath. "You talk too much," she told him.

"Maybe you don't talk enou—"

He didn't get an opportunity to finish. Kait had taken matters into her own hands again, just as she had yesterday, and she pressed her mouth against his, terminating any further flow of words on his part and eliminating the need for answering questions on hers.

An hour and a half later, after a third go-round had left them both spent and trying to steady their erratic breathing, Kait thrilled to the feel of Tom drawing his fingers along her hair with long, languid strokes. Shivers raced up and down her spine in response.

Though she knew the danger of letting her guard down, of allowing herself to simply savor this moment, Kait did just that and could feel contentment slipping in.

"About that question I asked earlier..." Tom began, whispering the words into her hair.

Her mind was a total blank right now. "What question?"

"About your last name."

Oh, right. That question. She shifted slightly so that she could look at him. "So you don't believe in maintaining an aura of mystery?"

"I believe in learning things about you," he told her, playing with a strand of her hair. "Lots of things. Significant things. Insignificant things..."

She made a small, hopefully disparaging sound. "You certainly have a lot of prerequisites for a casual-sex partner."

Her words hit him square in his chest. Tom rose up on his elbow and looked at her, his expression deadly serious. "What about this felt casual to you?" he asked.

That was just the problem. It hadn't. Not to her. To her what had just happened had been not just intense but very, very personal. And profound.

In her heart she knew that she was setting herself up for a fall.

Kait took a breath as she looked at the man beside her for a long moment.

Maybe the question he'd asked wasn't all *that* personal. After all, she wasn't ashamed of being adopted. It had marked the beginning of her life, really.

What would it hurt, telling Tom?

Telling him wouldn't actually be letting out some secret. He could look up the records, find out for himself if he pulled a few strings. Something that would be easy enough for him to do if he wanted to. So either he was just teasing her, being lazy—or he wanted her to tell him herself for whatever reason.

She knew what sort of a reason he was thinking of: that she trusted him enough to be personal with him. Because even more personal than sharing her body would be sharing her thoughts, her past.

This would take a giant leap on her part.

Kait took a deep breath—and leaped.

"Ronald Two Feathers had initially been part of a sting operation. My grandmother was given custody of me right after my mother gave birth. Seems someone, much to my mother's relief, thought prison wasn't the best place to raise a baby. That same line of thinking seemed to dictate that a grandmother would be the right person to raise a baby."

She stared at the ceiling. Truth be told, she had very faint memories of a tall, skinny, sharp-tongued woman who smelled of stale cigarette smoke and sweat.

"Except that the powers that be who decided my fate didn't know my grandmother." Kait laughed shortly.

"She was a resourceful woman and found uses for me from the very start."

Tom wasn't sure he understood what she meant. "Uses?"

Kait nodded. This, too, she vaguely remembered, mainly in bits and pieces. "If you're shoplifting food to feed your baby granddaughter, most store owners won't press charges and they're most likely to take pity on you and let you walk away with even more than you initially shoplifted.

"But after a while, my grandmother and her boy-friend found they needed drugs more than they needed food, so she tried to sell me."

"Sell you?" Tom echoed, horrified and incensed at the same time. She hadn't mentioned this part when she'd told him how she'd gotten her last name. Granted, he knew things like selling children went on, but he'd never had any personal contact with that sort of a case.

He was beginning to see why she had taken Megan's abduction so personally. Because she put herself in the little girl's place.

"My grandmother never had much luck. The first guy she tried to sell me to not only turned her down but he called the police. Ronald and his partner posed as a couple who desperately wanted a baby girl."

She vividly remembered the first time she saw Ronald Two Feathers. He looked impossibly tall, impossibly strong. He'd had shining blue-black hair and she thought he was a guardian angel, sent down to rescue her. Her four-year-old heart had fallen in love with him that very moment.

"My grandmother was more than happy to offer me to them—for fifty thousand dollars. The second the exchange was made, my grandmother and her boyfriend were taken into custody. They turned on each other in record time and were both sent to prison. I never saw my grandmother again.

"I was a scared, dirty, hungry little girl. Ronald bought me clothes, took me home." The corners of her mouth curved as she remembered. "Had his partner clean me up. And then he cooked me the first decent meal I'd had since I couldn't remember when—my grandmother thought my looking like a thin waif was more marketable," she explained.

"When social services came to take me away the next day, I cried and screamed and hung on to his leg. I didn't want to leave him. He promised he'd come visit me every chance he could—and, amazingly, he kept his word. He was always there, looking out for me, taking me to amusement parks, promising me that someday, he would give me a real home. Then one day he brought around this woman, told me he was getting married. I was twelve at the time and thought that would be the end of it. That he'd forget about me and I'd be on my own again." She closed her eyes and struggled to keep the hurtful memories at arm's length. "Some of the foster homes were pretty terrible.

"But Ronald Two Feathers was a man of his word. The first thing he and his new wife, Winona, did when they got back from their honeymoon was sign up to be foster parents and request that I be put in their care. I couldn't believe it." She closed her eyes again, willing herself not to cry. "I felt safe for the first time in years. Ronald and Winona adopted me before the year was out."

And that qualified as the happiest day of her life. But

it took her a long time to get over the fear that her new life was just temporary. That her grandmother would come back and take her away. Or that one of the foster parents she'd had over the years would materialize to steal her back and put her through hell again.

When she finally allowed herself to feel secure, fate came and stole it all away from her.

Tom heard the tears in her voice even though she maintained a stoic expression as she related her story for him. "And so you became Kaitlyn Two Feathers," he said, silently urging her to continue.

She smiled at that. "And so I became Kaitlyn Two Feathers."

"What was your last name before then?" he asked, curious.

She turned her head toward him. "I really can't remember." It was true, she really couldn't. She had absolutely no sense of curiosity when it came to that. She didn't want to know. "And as far as I'm concerned, I didn't exist before I was twelve and Ronald gave me a life."

He made a natural assumption. "Is he the reason you became a cop?" She nodded in response. "He must have been very proud of you."

He knew how his father had felt about his being part of the force. How he felt about all of them joining up. While Sean had had a father's natural fears, he was exceedingly proud of all of them.

"He was." Kait paused for a moment. It was always hard for her to say this. Still hard for her to come to terms with what her reality was. "Like I told you the other day, my father died four years ago. Cancer."

"And Winona?"

"She was in a terrible car accident less than a year after that. A sports car jumped the divider, plowed right into her." She pressed her lips together and stared at the ceiling again without seeing it at all. She blew out a shaky breath, trying to steady herself enough to continue. "She never woke up from that. Doctors told me she was brain-dead. I was the only next of kin she had, which meant that I had to be the one who told the doctors to pull the plug and terminate her life support. I struggled with that for a whole week, then realized I was just being selfish, trying to keep her alive for me, not because I honestly thought she could recover.

"I knew in my heart that she wouldn't have wanted to continue like that, a shell of the woman she'd been. So I said goodbye and told the doctor to turn off the machine." The sigh that escaped her lips was ragged. "She lived a whole twenty-three minutes after the machines stopped. And then she died."

Tom thought he'd never heard a voice as sad as Kait's as she said that.

And then she tried to brighten a little, pushing all the emotions away into a small, invisible container where she kept them locked up. "I'm sure Ronald was waiting for her on the other side. She'd really been only half alive after he died."

Tom leaned over her and brushed away the tears that zigzagged down the side of her face, staining her cheek and the pillow beneath her. "I am very, very sorry you had to go through that, Kait."

She took another deep breath. It really didn't help all that much.

"Yeah, so am I." She found she had to take a second breath before she could continue speaking. Her throat felt tight and she had to push the words out. She looked at him, trying desperately to regain her equilibrium. "Are you satisfied now?" she added. "Is that a good enough explanation for you about my last name?"

She was in pain, Tom thought, and more than anything, he wanted to absorb that pain, take it away from her. But all he could do was slip his arm around her and draw her closer to him.

"I'm sorry," he repeated quietly. "I didn't mean for you to bring up all this pain," he confessed, then whispered, "Thank you for letting me in," and he pressed a kiss to her temple.

She curled into him even as she balked at his undoing her. "Don't be nice to me, Tom. When you're nice to me, you make me want to cry. And I hate to cry."

He knew even that admission had been extremely personal for her. "I could kick you if that made you feel better," he offered.

"Well, what I'd really rather—"

The phone on his nightstand rang, cutting into her thoughts. She turned her head toward it as he reached to answer it.

"What I'd really like," she concluded, switching directions, "is to pull that damn thing right out of the wall."

Tom held his hand up, the gesture asking for her silence, as he tried to make out the voice on the other end of the line.

Halfway into the first shaky sentence, he recognized it. It was the clerk from the car-rental agency. Every nerve ending Tom had went on the alert.

"I called like you told me to, Detective. That white van you were asking about? Well, I just saw it. It's back on the lot."

Chapter 13

The expression on Tom's face told Kait something was definitely up. If the call had been inconsequential, he would have hung up by now.

Was that Andrew requesting a return audience tomorrow or in the near future? When they'd been there, she'd heard the man talking about throwing another party for Christmas Eve, which was only a few days away.

Kait could hear the clock in her head ticking away the minutes. She'd promised Amanda that she'd have Megan back to her by then.

Or maybe the caller was his Uncle Brian. Maybe the chief of detectives had found out that she was operating on her own out here, without the blessings of Lt. Blackwell. In order for him to have found that out, he had either decided to call her lieutenant to check her out or—

"We'll be right there. Don't go anywhere," Tom ordered sharply.

Kait braced herself, just in case. "We'll be right where?" she asked, watching his face carefully.

Tom dropped the receiver into the cradle and got to his feet. It was obvious that he'd meant what he said about getting to the unknown destination as quickly as possible.

Picking up his jeans from the floor, he told her, "That was the clerk from the car-rental agency."

If he hadn't had her attention before, he did now. Kait scrambled out of bed, taking her cue from him. Her clothes were lying in the doorway.

"At this hour?" she questioned. "Why would he be opened now?" It didn't make sense. "Who rents a car at close to midnight?"

Tom looked around for the blue pullover he'd worn earlier, before clothing had no longer been an option. Spotting a blue cuff peeking out from under the bed, he pulled the shirt out.

He shook off the dust, pushed his arms through the sleeves and pulled the shirt on. "According to him, he lives near the place and he was out walking his dog when he decided to look in on the lot to make sure nobody had broken in to steal any of the cars." Dressed, he began to hunt for his shoes. "Not only had no one stolen any of the vehicles, but according to him, the van was back. My guess is that it must have been returned after he closed down tonight."

Kait was hurrying into her own clothes as she listened. Questions multiplied in her head. Trust was something she usually held in abeyance. "Doesn't that strike you as a little odd? Bringing the van back when no one was around?"

He knew what she was thinking. That maybe the rental clerk was in on the abduction after all and had just played dumb. But if that were the case, why the improbable story about the van's sudden return? Why not just have the van returned on someone else's watch, when he wasn't on duty?

After turning the thought over in his head, Tom had another explanation.

"Not if you think about it," he said. He sat down on the edge of the bed and began to pull on the worn pair of boots he'd tugged off earlier. "The guy who took Megan is probably afraid that it's only a matter of time before someone sees the van and connects him to the abduction. Afraid he's going to run out of luck, he brings the vehicle back. One less thing to worry about."

She supposed that made sense. In a way. "Until we get the fingerprints off the inside of the vehicle."

"We already got those, remember?" he reminded her, thinking of the application form that had been dusted. "The guy's squeaky-clean."

The hell he was. "Yeah, a squeaky-clean predator," she said bitterly. "I've been thinking about the case and it seems to me that this has to be a two-man job. Someone to drive the van and someone to grab the girl." She saw that he was about to voice his doubts and she talked right over him, convinced that she was right.

"Think about it. If he's the only one, he has to grab the girl, stick her into the van, then run to the driver's side and drive away. Too risky that way and too time-consuming. Megan was taken from her front yard in broad daylight. There had to be two people involved. And maybe the second guy got careless, left his prints on the dashboard, or the door panel. All we need is one clear print if the guy has a record somewhere." She looked at Tom, silently asking him to humor her. "It's all we've got."

He nodded after a moment. What she'd just said made sense. And who knew? Maybe they would finally get lucky with this case.

"You're right," he told her. He grabbed his wallet and car keys off the bureau. "Let's go."

They arrived at the car-rental agency in record time. A very nervous-looking Clark was pacing back and forth before the dark office. An equally jumpy-looking Chihuahua tethered to a leash kept pace with him.

The moment Clark saw the white Crown Victoria approaching, he tensed, his drawn face looking even more pasty in the light from the streetlamp. It was apparent that he was eager to go home and put all this behind him as quickly as possible.

"It's back here, I'll show you," he offered eagerly, then hurried away without waiting.

"Was there any footage of the van being brought back?" Kait asked. Maybe this time, the man hadn't kept his face so hidden. If they had a clearer picture to work with, maybe someone would recognize him.

"No, sorry," Clark said. "Camera broke down right after you left. The boss is real mad. He just got that one on eBay about three months ago. Said you can't trust anyone these days," the clerk complained, shaking his head.

"So, no tape," Tom repeated. He found that just too much of a fortunate coincidence. Entering the lot, they made their way over to the white van. It was the only one there. "Just the van," he said as they stood in front of it. The vehicle had recently been washed. There didn't appear to be a speck of dust on it. He frowned. "Probably no fingerprints, either."

"We don't know that," Kait insisted, for once refusing to relinquish hope. "We get this to the lab, have them go over every inch of the van to see if—" She stopped talking abruptly, then said, "Oh, damn."

Tom looked around, searching for what had just caused her to stop midsentence. He saw nothing out of the ordinary. "What?"

"Tomorrow's Sunday," she lamented. Every time she was ready to go flying out of the gate, something stopped her and held her back. "There's not going to be anyone working at the lab—is there?" she asked, prepared for a negative reply, hoping for a positive one.

"The lab's usually closed on a Sunday," Tom said, confirming her fears. And then he smiled. "But you forget, I've got an in with the head of the day unit," he said with a wink.

His father. How could she have forgotten that? "You think he'll come down if we ask him to?" she asked, holding her breath.

The answer to that was a resounding yes. "When my dad was a kid, one of his sisters—or one of the little girls he *thought* was his sister at the time—was abducted. No ransom note, nothing. She was gone for months. The family pretty much gave up all hope of ever finding her."

He'd heard the story more than a few times when he was growing up, first as a warning to be careful not to trust strangers, and later on as a reaffirmation about the positive things that happened in life—as well as the reason why his father became part of the police force.

"But it turned out she was one of the lucky ones, thanks to the relentless efforts of the detective who caught the case. His name, by the way, was Seamus Cavanaugh."

She looked at him in disbelief. But he didn't appear to be pulling her leg. "Was that—"

Tom nodded. "Yeah, the man who turned out to be Dad's real father."

Kait could only shake her head in wonder. "Talk about it being a small world..."

"Yeah, I know," he said with a laugh. That had always been his mother's favorite line. He could only think how she would have reacted to the past couple of months. No doubt she would have been stunned. And, most likely, echoing the line over and over again. "So, to answer your initial question, yeah, I'm pretty damn sure I can get my father to come out and open up the lab. I'm equally sure that he'll go over the car with a fine-tooth comb. If there's a fingerprint to be found, he'll find it."

With that, Tom took out his cell phone to call his father.

Kait turned toward the clerk, who seemed to be growing more and more antsy.

The moment she looked in his direction, he blurted out, "Can I go home now?"

She could understand his wanting to go home, but the man was sweating. And it was exceedingly cold tonight. Her eyes narrowed.

"Is something wrong, Clark?" she asked him, watching his face.

"No." He glanced around uneasily, then seemed to almost huddle closer to her if not actually against her. "Why do you think there's something wrong?"

"Well, for one thing, you're fidgeting," she pointed out. "Any particular reason for that?"

"Yeah," he bit off, agitated. "According to you, whoever drove that van is a kidnapper. He might not take kindly to my calling you about the van. What if he comes back and sees me talking to the police? He'll kill me, I just know it!"

She sincerely doubted that the man would be back, not if he went through all this trouble to get rid of the van in the dead of night in order to erase any connection between it and him. But the rental clerk was almost jumping out of his skin and she took pity on him.

"If he does come back, you call us right away and then get as far away from here as possible," she advised in as calm a voice as she could. "But I wouldn't worry about him if I were you. We're bound to get him, and when we do he'll be going away for a very long time. The last thing on his mind will be the rental agency and you."

Clark looked at her, a wide-eyed puppy. "You think you'll get him?"

"Thanks to you, yes, we'll get him." *And when we do, I'm going to get him to tell me where Megan is even if I have to beat it out of him,* she added silently.

The clerk's agitated, microscopic pet had been barking at Tom and at her nonstop since they'd arrived. She looked at the nervous man now and asked, "What's your pet's name?"

"Killer," he told her.

"Of course it is," she murmured under her breath.

If ever a name didn't fit a pet, this was it. But he made so much noise, she could barely hear herself think. And Tom was still on the phone, trying to hear what was being said on the other end of the line.

Kait crouched down and held her hand out to the animal in a nonthreatening manner. She let the dog sniff first her fingertips, then her hand before she made the attempt to pet the animal.

When she did, Killer instantly flopped down on his side, waiting to be petted some more.

"He doesn't usually do that," Clark said, mystified at his pet's reaction.

"I'm pretty good with animals," she told him as she rubbed the dog's small stomach. At least he'd stopped barking, she silently congratulated herself.

The dog shifted so that he was completely on his back, his little paws held up as if begging. And in a manner of speaking, he was. He presented Kait more of an area to rub.

Kait laughed softly. What she'd told the rental clerk was true. She was good with animals. She had an affinity for them, especially the ones that had been turned loose to wander the streets, hungry, or the ones that had been badly abused before they'd been thrown out.

She could relate to both their survival instincts and to the basic distrust they harbored. Some hands were ready to strike rather than offer friendship.

"He'll be here in twenty minutes," Tom announced, terminating his call and slipping the cell phone back into his pocket. "He's bringing Della-Vega. Della-Vega will get the van to the lab," he added, realizing that the name probably meant nothing to her. "They'll go over it there. He promised to call if there was any news."

Kait nodded, pleased. And then she asked a little uneasily, "Was he annoyed?"

Tom could not remember ever seeing his father annoyed. The man was far too even-tempered for that.

"As it happens, he was still up," he told her. "He'd just come home from the party a couple of minutes before I called—and my dad knows that I wouldn't just call him at this hour to shoot the breeze, so, no, he wasn't angry. Just surprised that the van was brought back at all. He said that it would have been a lot easier for the guy if he'd just had the van go over a cliff."

Kait had already explored that avenue. The only conclusion she reached was that maybe someone in on the abduction was ordinarily a law-abiding citizen the way they'd guessed when the prints hadn't come up in any database. Law-abiding citizens didn't destroy others' property if they could help it.

But then, she reminded herself, they didn't get involved in the abduction of little girls, either. So what was going on here? The further they got in the case, the less clear things seemed to get.

Her head really began to ache as she jumped from theory to theory, not knowing which to embrace and which to abandon. What they desperately needed were leads.

She prayed that Tom's father would be able to give them some.

Tom noticed the strained look that crossed her face. "Headache?" he asked.

He'd gotten it right on the first guess, she thought. The man read her far too easily. And that little habit made her very *un*easy.

"I'm working on one," she told him.

"I've got some Aspirin in the car," he volunteered. He saw the question enter her eyes and explained, "I get pretty achy after sitting in the car for twelve hours on a stakeout."

She nodded, grateful for the offer. "Aspirin sounds great."

"So is it okay if I go now?" the rental clerk asked again. He'd picked up his pet, and with the animal pressed against his chest he looked ready to go— quickly.

Tom glanced in the man's direction. He'd almost forgotten about the mousy clerk. But rather than give the man the go-ahead, he glanced at Kait instead. This was her show.

"Can he go?" he asked her.

For her part, Kait was surprised that the detective, one of those men who seemed to thrive on his masculinity, deferred to her.

She liked that.

"I've got no further use for him right now," she answered. "So, yes, it's okay."

"You can go," Tom told the clerk in case the man had missed that.

Man and dog were gone in a flash.

"You know," Tom speculated, leading the way around to the front of the dark rental office again, "if I didn't know better, I'd say that mousy little clerk was setting us up for something."

She told him why she'd already dismissed that theory. "I think he's too cowardly for that. My guess is that what he said is true—he's afraid the guy who took the van might still be watching for some reason and he doesn't really want to be seen with us. He reminds me of the type who's afraid of his own shadow—literally."

Kait scanned the area slowly, taking everything in, from the scattered parked cars, all apparently empty, to the vacant, darkened stores, denuded of their signs and placed up for rent. The area appeared desolate and deserted.

"But, just in case," she said, "do you have your gun with you?"

He grinned easily, his eyes indicating his right leg. The weapon was strapped on there, beneath his jeans. "Never leave home without it."

They had that in common. The smile she offered in return was tense around the edges. "Me, neither."

"You know, it might be really sexy," Tom suggested, trying to break up the tension, "seeing you wearing just your weapon and nothing else—except maybe your high heels."

She laughed at the image. To do that would have made her feel far too vulnerable. "In your dreams, Cavanaugh."

"Yup," he agreed, his eyes glimmering. "That about sums it up."

His vehicle was still parked at the curb, right in front of the rental agency. He unlocked the passenger side and then opened the door. Reaching in, he opened up the glove compartment and took out a small greenish plastic bottle. It was half-empty.

"There you go," he said, handing her the bottle. He watched as she shook out two pills. "Now all we have to do is find you some water so that you can swallow those d—"

He was about to say "down" but found that he didn't

need to. Neither did he need to look for water or any other liquid for that matter. As he watched her, Kait had popped the pills into her mouth, leaned her head back and then swallowed.

Tom could feel the small white tablets sticking in his throat even though he hadn't been the one doing the swallowing.

"Did you just swallow those dry?" he asked her in disbelief.

Replacing the top, Kait handed the bottle back to him. "Uh-huh."

"And they're not stuck in your throat?" he asked incredulously.

The corners of her mouth curved a tiny bit as she said, "Nope."

If it had been him, he would have choked. He found he usually needed an entire full glass of water whenever he had to down any pills.

"You are a woman of many hidden talents," Tom marveled.

She laughed at the expression on his face. "You don't know the half of it."

"No," he readily agreed, then thought back to what the rental clerk's phone call earlier had interrupted. The talents he'd uncovered already were pretty provocative. "But I'd like to."

It was just empty, distracting talk, she told herself. He didn't mean anything by it, and she would do well to remember that and not take his words seriously.

Certainly not to heart the way she so badly wanted to.

This had no future.

They had no future.

With just a thimbleful of luck, she and Tom would be closing in on the kidnapper soon. And, one way or the other, they would find Megan. Once they did, her time here would be over. She had no reason to remain in Aurora. Her job—and her life, such as it was—was back in New Mexico. His job, as well as his enormous family, was out here.

What she'd found in the dark, in his arms, no matter how wonderful, would all be part of her past in the blink of an eye.

She had to remember that.

Chapter 14

"So, were you able to find any decent fingerprints?" Kait asked hopefully.

It was several hours later. Once secured, the van had been towed to the lab and brought in via an underground, back entrance. She'd tried to pace herself in order to give her partner's father enough time to go over the vehicle. She didn't want the man to think she was breathing down his neck, even though, in effect, that was exactly what she was doing.

Belatedly, she realized that she was thinking of Tom as her partner, not just someone she was temporarily working with. When had that happened? She pushed the question from her mind. Answering wouldn't help anything. In fact, it might even make things worse. Life had suddenly gotten very complicated.

Rather than return back to Tom's place, she'd opted

to go to the squad room and review the list of known child predators that they had already interviewed once. She was looking for some small nugget of information that she and Tom might have missed the first time and that would, once noted, eventually lead her to the answer and the man she was searching for.

Because she stayed at the precinct, so did Tom. Above her loudly voiced protests, he divided the list between them and then engaged in the same careful reexamination that she was conducting.

Unfortunately, he was also coming up with the same answer: nothing.

When she announced that she was taking a break and going down to the basement to see if his father was having any better luck than they were, he'd been more than happy to take a break with her.

Kait's question now hung in the air. Sean looked up from his microscope. His sharp blue eyes shifted from Kait to his son.

"Any prints?" he echoed, and then laughed shortly. He was knee-deep in them. "We've got tons of prints. Take your pick."

She tried to reconcile what he was telling her with the fact that the van had been brought back in the dead of night so that the driver could avoid detection—or at least so she had thought.

"The men who took Megan didn't bother wiping down the inside of the van?" Kait asked incredulously. That didn't make any sense at all.

"I think it was more of a case that they were hoping to have their prints lost in the crowd. Or maybe I'm just giving them too much credit," he allowed. "Maybe they just didn't think about having their fingerprints being traced back to them."

"In this day and age?" Tom asked in disbelief. "Don't these people watch TV?"

There was a hell of a lot on TV these days, not like when he was a boy and the choices were limited, Sean thought.

"Maybe they're more into reality shows than procedurals," the older man theorized. "Whatever the reason, so far I've come across about fifteen sets of prints. I'm running as many through the database as I can at one time. Here are the first matches." He picked up several pages that he'd printed out and offered the lot to the young woman. "Good luck."

"Thanks," Kait said, mentally crossing her fingers that this time, they would find something. "And thanks for coming in on a Sunday."

"If we find that little girl, it'll be more than worth it," Sean told her. With that, he lowered his eyes and got back to work.

The print matches had all come with names and current addresses. Armed with that, she and Tom set out to track down the abductors, praying that the men they were after weren't something else, as well.

"You look dead on your feet."

Kait had collapsed onto the passenger seat in his car after yet another one of the matches Sean Cavanaugh and his CSI lab had provided had turned out to be someone with an alibi for the afternoon that Megan had been taken from her front yard.

For a moment, she hadn't even heard what Tom said

to her and then she replayed his words in her head. His assessment was way too accurate.

"Bet you say that to all the girls," she murmured.

"Only the ones who've been up for a day and a half," he quipped. "Why don't we knock off for today and go to bed?" he proposed. When she raised a skeptical eyebrow at his suggestion, he clarified, "*Really* go to bed." Because, as enticing as she'd proved to be, he was pretty beat himself right now.

"Just this last one," she said, holding up the last match that Tom's father had given them. She was determined to see this through. "Your dad's been at it as long as we have, and this is the last set of prints he matched. Wouldn't seem right if we just set it aside until tomorrow."

"Right," Tom said stoically, not so much agreeing as resigning himself to the stubborn woman's need to follow through. And he didn't want her going alone, even though he knew that she was perfectly capable of going solo. God knew she'd told him about it enough times. "Might as well find out that this one is a dead end, too."

Somewhere along the line, their roles had gotten reversed, Kait thought. Now she was the one who clung to hope. "I thought you were an optimist."

"I am." He took the sheet from her and oriented himself as to the address. This last set of prints belonged to a woman. He tried to keep an open mind. "Until after the thirty-sixth hour. After that, my darker side has a tendency to come out."

"Thanks for the warning." They'd stopped by the precinct to see if Sean had managed to find any other matches, and he had given them this last name. Kait felt as if she'd never even left the car. "You don't have to come with me, you know."

For the umpteenth time that day, Tom started up the Crown Victoria. "We've got one car between us, so yes, I do."

"You've got four million Cavanaughs you could call to give you a ride home," she pointed out.

"Just shut up and put on your seat belt," he instructed. "Besides," he continued once they were both buckled up and he began to pull out of the parking space, "who's going to cover your back if you go alone?"

"You mean protect me from—" She paused for a moment as she looked down at the mug shot in her possession. "—Greta Crammer?" The subject of this last interview was a heavyset woman who looked older than her thirty-eight years. "I think I can take her. Especially if I bring a bottle of whiskey with me."

According to the information under the mug shot, the woman had been picked up on suspicion of drunken driving more than a decade ago. If not for that, Sean would have had nothing that served as a match for her prints.

"It's been eleven years," Tom pointed out, glancing at the sheet. "She might have sworn off drinking in that time."

"Or she might have just been lucky and hasn't gotten caught a second time," Kait guessed.

"There's that," he agreed. As they pulled out of the parking lot and onto the street, he glanced at her face. He couldn't quite read her expression. "What?"

"What—what?" Kait fired back at him, confused. Maybe she *was* getting too punchy. But she had an odd feeling about this one. Something told her that she'd regret it if she put this off until tomorrow.

"Something about this one speak to you?" Tom asked. "Because you've got a really strange expression on your face."

She didn't want him pinning her down like that. Besides, he'd probably find it funny and she didn't want him laughing at her. So she shrugged as she said evasively, "Probably just indigestion from that pizza you picked up. Pineapples do not belong anywhere near a pizza, much less on it," she told him firmly.

Tom laughed at her argument. "Didn't know you were a pizza expert among all your other talents. Nobody forced you to eat the pineapple chunks," he reminded her. "You could have easily picked them off."

"Seriously, though. Do you have a feeling about this one? Tell me," he coaxed. He was a great believer in gut feelings.

"So you can laugh at me?" she challenged. "No, thanks."

Tired, he blew out an impatient breath. "Kait, I'm chasing around dead-end leads all day Sunday when I could be sleeping in. I dragged my father down here to work the case. Does it look like I'm looking for a laugh?"

"No," she said quietly.

He understood that she was defensive because of her background, but at this point, he would have thought that he'd proved himself to her.

"When are you finally going to put that chip of yours away for good?" he asked. "Or are you just going to keep whipping it out every time you take offense when none is intended?"

"You're right," she admitted, even though it cost her. "I should be thanking you."

"I'm not asking you to thank me, I'm asking you to trust me. We're on the same team, the same side, so stop jumping away every time you think I'm going to say something and turn on you. Get it through your head—I'm not, okay?"

"Okay."

With that hopefully cleared up, he returned to his original question. "Now, do you have a hunch about this, or are we just clearing the board so we can start fresh in the morning?"

"I've got a hunch," she admitted. "A strong one. And I can't even tell you why." That was the worst part. She couldn't explain why this certain feeling fluttered in her stomach.

"You're a cop, you don't need a reason why. It's something that comes with the territory," he told her in all seriousness. "Last hunch I had kept my partner from blowing up."

Despite how tired she felt, she looked at him, his last comment cutting through her fatigue. "What happened?" she asked.

But he waved the question away. He didn't like bragging, and to tell her the story where he was the hero would be bragging.

"Story for another time," was all he said. "According to the address on that arrest report, we're almost there," he commented, slowing the car down to less than the speed limit while he took in his surroundings.

The residential area was a complete antithesis to the neighborhood they'd been in at the rental agency just before midnight. There, a person would have been afraid to go out after dark, even if they were armed. Here, he had a feeling a person was safe even if he had hundred-dollar bills hanging out of his pockets.

"Looks like Greta Crammer has done well for herself," he commented.

The GPS arrow on his screen—he'd deliberately muted the voice command because he found it grating—pointed to the right, then to the left. The houses they passed, all two-story, were absolutely huge, not a single modest home in the bunch.

"What do you do with so much space?" Tom marveled under his breath as he passed a large house.

"How long does it take to clean a place like that?" she asked as they drove by a residence with a stone front that looked as if it was meant to be a castle, not simply someone's home.

"You got a house like that, you don't worry about cleaning it. You pay someone to do the work," he quipped.

He thought it was a waste of time coming here, she could see it in his eyes. But he was humoring her, which meant a lot. She wouldn't have been able to sleep, thinking about this last one.

Part of her wanted this ordeal—searching for Megan—to finally be over.

Another part of her—the selfish part—wanted it never to end. Because it would mean not just the end to the search, but an end to everything else.

You're supposed to be ready for that, remember? she upbraided herself.

"This is it," Tom announced, pulling up at the curb in front of a Tudor-style house.

I certainly hope so, Kait thought as she got out. She heard the car's doors shutting rhythmically.

Kait started to head toward the front door of the house, but at the last moment she detoured over to the gate that led into the backyard.

"What are you doing?" Tom asked. Had she heard something?

"Listen," she hissed, her own voice low.

Drawing closer, he cocked his head. When he did, he heard a high-pitched voice saying the word "No," over and over again.

Just as a child would.

He lengthened his stride, getting ahead of Kait, and pushed open the gate.

A startled woman—an older version of the photograph that Kait had—and an unhappy girl who'd obviously been crying looked in their direction. The little girl had extremely short blond hair. Both were caught by surprise.

The little girl's eyes widened, as if recognizing Kait. She gave every indication that she was about to run toward them, but the woman quickly grabbed her and pulled her back. With both hands laid over the small child's shoulders, she anchored her in place.

Tom quickly scanned the area. The entire yard looked like a child's idea of paradise. There was an elaborate playhouse, an extensive swing set and a host of other things throughout the yard. Everything a child could possibly wish for was right here in this fairy-tale place.

The next moment, a stocky, gray-haired man who'd been standing in the back of the yard quickly stepped forward. The expression on his florid face went from concern to the embodiment of dismay.

"Can I help you?" he asked, his tone of voice polite, but far from pleased at this sudden invasion.

Kait's eyes widened as the man moved so that his body was in front of the hostile-looking woman and the child she was holding on to.

"Tom."

Though she said nothing else, he knew she was asking him if he saw what she did: the resemblance between the photo they had and the man standing before them. It took him less than a moment. There was no doubt in his mind. "Yeah, I see it."

"See what?" the man demanded, looking from one to the other, his voice growing more tense, as was his body language.

"Kaitlyn, I want to go home," the little girl suddenly cried, trying to jerk free of the woman's hold on her. "Take me home," she pleaded.

"You *are* home," the woman snapped.

"You're the guy who rented a white van several weeks ago," Tom said.

The man's eyes shifted from one to the other as if he was waiting for something. "You've made a mistake," he insisted. His voice quavered.

"I don't think we have," Tom answered, his tone deliberately mild.

The man grew more nervous. "I think I'd like you to leave," he said. "You're scaring my little girl. If you don't go, I'll, I'll call the police," he threatened.

"We are the police," Tom told him. He took out his badge and held it up for the other man to see.

The moment he did, Greta Crammer yanked the little

girl closer to her. "Come inside, Sally, it's time for your bath."

"I don't want to go with you," the little girl cried, digging her feet in. "I want my mommy."

"Don't be ridiculous. I am your mommy," Greta snapped angrily. "Now come inside with me. Do as I tell you!"

Kait instantly moved toward the woman and the child. "I don't think so, Greta," she said to the other woman.

As she went to separate the little girl from the woman, the latter sharply yanked the little girl's arms, pulling her even closer. The child screamed.

"Don't touch my daughter!" Greta cried, hysteria building in her voice. "You can't have her! I'm not going to lose her again, do you hear me?"

Then the girl began to cry pitifully.

Her pretty brown hair had been chopped off and dyed, but it was Megan. Thank God it was Megan, Kait thought. "Megan," Kait began in a calming voice. "Your mommy sent me to bring you home." Megan raised her head to look at her. "It's going to be all right."

That was when Greta snatched up the pair of pruning shears that had been left out on the glass-top table. A wild look in her brown eyes, she held the shears like a weapon against Megan's throat.

"You take a step closer and I'll kill her. I swear I'll kill her and myself. I'm not going to lose my baby again, do you hear me?" she shrieked. "Not again. She's mine!"

"Sir," Tom began in a low, calm voice that belied the anxious feeling that was in the pit of his stomach, "is this woman your wife?"

"Yes, yes she is. She's not well. Please don't hurt her." Greta Crammer's husband looked terrified.

"Then tell your wife to let the little girl go before she does get hurt," Tom advised.

"Greta, please," the man begged, but his pleas fell on deaf ears.

"No, Max!" Greta snapped. "She's mine. She came back to me and I won't let her go. I can't. Make them go away, Max," she begged. "Make them go away."

"We don't want anyone to get hurt today," Tom told Max since he was obviously the more reasonable of the two. Then he looked at Greta and said, "Drop the scissors, ma'am."

Kait glanced toward Tom and saw that he had drawn his service revolver. He pointed the weapon directly at Greta Crammer's head.

The desperate look in Greta's eyes made everything click into place for Kait. She understood. "You lost your little girl, didn't you Greta?"

Greta swallowed as if the painful memory threatened to choke her.

"Ten years ago," she answered. "She ran into the street to get her ball. The driver should have seen her. But she was so little. I begged her not to die, but she wouldn't listen. But it's okay now, because she came back to me. She came back," she cried happily, looking down at the child who wasn't hers. "I found her again."

"No, you didn't," Kait stressed. "Your little girl's gone. This is Megan Willows and she doesn't belong to you."

"Yes, she does!" Greta screamed. The sound was bloodcurdling.

"Her mother desperately wants her back, Greta,"

Kait told her, keeping her voice low, nonthreatening. "You remember what that's like, don't you? To feel like your heart's been torn out of your chest and then mangled into little tiny pieces. Please let Megan go back to her mother."

"Her name's not Megan, it's Sally. This is Sally," Greta insisted. "My Sally. This is *my* Sally." With each word, her voice grew louder, until she was all but shrieking.

"No, I'm not," the child cried pitifully. "I'm Megan. My name's Megan. And you're not my mommy!"

The other woman began to sob in frustration. Her hand went lax and the pruning shears dropped from her fingers. "I just want my baby. I can't live without my baby," she cried. "Please don't take her away from me again. Max, don't let them do this," she begged her husband, turning toward him.

Kait took advantage of the moment. Moving swiftly, she wrested the child away from Greta's grip.

"No!" Greta cried in horror. "Give her back to me. Please, please give her back to me!"

As she held the little girl against her, Kait watched the heavyset woman fall to the ground in a sobbing, incoherent heap.

Megan turned her head away and buried it against Kait's hip. The little girl clung to her for all she was worth. Kait could feel the little girl trembling against her.

"It's over, Megan, it's over," she whispered over and over again.

And, as her heart both sank and was elated, Kait knew that it was.

Chapter 15

What happened next seemed like a giant jumble.

When she looked back at the events later, Kait still had trouble pulling apart the various strands in order to make sense of it all and replay what happened in its proper order.

There was no order, no clarity.

If she could have actually put it into words at all, she would have had to say that it was some gut instinct that warned her, that sent her into action before she ever knew what she was acting against—or for.

One moment it seemed as if it was all over. Megan had been recovered and the couple who had abducted her were about to be taken into custody. Max Crammer was in the process of being handcuffed by Tom.

Then out of nowhere came this enraged, guttural sound. It seemed almost disembodied, like a wild animal backed into a corner and putting up one last, desperate fight not to be taken captive.

The second Kait heard it, she quickly pushed Megan off to the side, out of range. Then she swung around and threw herself on top of Tom who, because he was slipping the cuffs on Max, had his back to what they both had taken for granted was a chastened, subdued and broken Greta Crammer.

Except that she wasn't any of those things.

As if a sudden surge of energy had infused itself through her the moment she saw her husband being taken into custody and her "daughter" pulled away from her, the woman lumbered to her feet, shears once again clutched in her hand. She hurdled herself at Tom's back, holding the shears aloft, ready to sink them in and kill the man who was about to kill her only dream.

She would have driven the blades right into his back if Kait hadn't knocked Tom down, putting her own back between the shears and their target.

Kait's involuntary scream echoed through the yard as the shear blades sank deep into her shoulder.

Horrified, Tom twisted out from beneath her, his weapon back in his hands. He discharged it twice, stopping the woman as she began to deliver a second, most likely fatal blow.

There was a stunned expression on Greta's face as she sank to her knees and then crumpled, blood oozing from the bullet wound in the middle of her forehead. The other bullet had caught her in the chest.

The woman was dead before she hit the ground.

Tom instantly turned to Kait, his heart hammering so hard it felt as if it was breaking apart his ribs. He'd never been so terrified in his life.

"Kait!"

Dazed, the yard shifting back and forth before her eyes, Kait struggled to get up on her knees. She didn't quite make it, but she waved him away. "I'm fine. We're even now. Go see about Megan," she ordered weakly.

Rather than cowering in a corner, the little girl came running over to Kait. Tears welled up in her eyes and streamed down her cheeks.

"You're hurt. Did she kill you?" she cried, clearly frightened but unwilling to back away from the woman who had rescued her.

"Nope… Takes…more than…that…to kill me." Despite her desire to reassure Megan by making light of the situation, Kate had to struggle to force each word out of her mouth. They emerged in slow motion.

In the background, she heard Tom yelling something into his cell phone that sounded like, "Officer down, officer down."

It took her a full moment to realize he was calling about her and not someone else.

"You're…safe now…Megan. She…can't…hurt… you."

It was the last thing Kait remembered saying. As she tried to lift her hand to stroke the little girl's hair, she felt everything pulling away from her.

And then it went completely dark.

Was she on fire?

The burning sensation that seared through her, encompassing her back, hurt like hell. As she tried to take in a breath, she found it hurt even more.

Disoriented, Kait tried to make out shapes. That was

when she realized that her eyes were shut. Opening them took almost all the strength she had.

What was going on here?

After what felt like an eternity, she finally did manage to open her eyes. Blinking, Kait slowly focused on her surroundings.

White.

Hospital bed.

She was lying in a hospital bed. Why? What was she doing here? And why did it hurt so much to breathe?

Kait struggled to sit up and found, to her everlasting exasperation, that she couldn't. She was just too weak and in too much pain to pick up more than just her head. "Damn it."

The whispered, vehement curse jolted Tom out of the semisleep that had slipped over him. With a start he realized that he must have finally lost the battle against complete exhaustion, a place he'd come to after pacing the length of the hallway, going to hell and back more times than he could count as he waited for Kait to come out of surgery.

When he saw her surgeon approaching, he'd pounced on the man, getting to him before he could even take down his surgical mask.

"She's a very lucky young woman," Dr. Meyers had told him, sharing the news with the throng of people who'd come to keep vigil once word had spread that Kait had been stabbed. "Less than a quarter of an inch lower and you'd be standing over her casket right now."

Brian had woven his way to his nephew and the surgeon. "Then she's going to be all right?" he asked.

Dr. Meyers nodded. "She's a strong woman. She'll be fine—as long as she gives herself some time to heal and doesn't jump right back into work." He looked at Brian knowingly. "I know how you people can be."

"We'll make sure she gets plenty of rest," Sean assured the physician, then looked at his son and smiled encouragingly. "She's a survivor, Tom. Everything about her says it."

Tom barely remembered nodding. Everything inside him quivered. Now that he knew she was going to live, all the emotions he'd been holding at bay exploded, threatening to decimate his knees.

"You want to go home and get some sleep?" Bridget asked, moving closer to him. "I'll stay with her until you get back."

"Or I can," he heard Kendra offer from the back of the crowd.

There was no way he was going to leave the hospital. Not until he saw Kait regain consciousness.

"No, that's okay. I want to be here when she opens her eyes." He looked at Brian. "That knife was intended for me. She put herself in harm's way for me." There was guilt and agony in every syllable.

He could tell by Brian's expression that he wasn't telling the chief of detectives anything that the man didn't already know.

Brian patted him on the shoulder. "Hell of a girl you've got there, Tom," he said with unabashed deep admiration.

He turned his attention to the people in the waiting room and beyond. All of them had gathered here to support Tom and the woman who had saved their cousin's life. Now that they knew she was going to pull through, it was time to give Tom a little space.

"Okay, let's clear out and give the man some breathing room," he told the others.

Out of the corner of his eye, Brian saw the relieved expression on one of the nurses' face. More than one had passed by the waiting room, trying to convince the group to wait for word in shifts, or to appoint just one person who could serve as a messenger. The suggestions fell on deaf ears. No one wanted to go home and leave Tom at a time like this.

Now they could.

As they filed out past Tom, each had something encouraging to say. Sean brought up the rear, telling his son to "Call one of us if you need anything, anything at all."

Tom merely nodded his compliance, too overcome to speak.

After his family had left, he'd gone to Kait's room to wait until the orderlies brought her up from the recovery area. When they came in and moved her bed into the room, all he could think of was that she looked almost as pale as the sheet that covered her. Her drained complexion was a sharp contrast to the bright red blood that had pooled around her torso back in the Crammers' yard.

He'd been content to just sit beside her bed and watch her sleep because now at least he knew that she would eventually wake up. Reassured, he could wait no matter how long it took.

Tom didn't remember falling asleep, but obviously, he must have. The hoarsely voiced curse had crossed over his threshold of sleep and pulled him across it.

He took a deep breath the moment his eyes flew open. "You're awake."

"Apparently," she mumbled.

He'd almost lost her. He hadn't realized how devastating that idea was until it had almost happened. Tom looked at her now, absorbing every nuance.

He wanted to take her hand in his, but he refrained. He didn't know if that would hurt her somehow and he couldn't chance it.

"How do you feel?"

It took her a second to find the words. "Like a semi ran me over three times and then the driver set me on fire." Why was it so tiring to talk? She felt incredibly exhausted. "What am I doing here?" she asked.

The sudden lump in his throat made it hard to talk. "Recovering from surgery."

Her eyebrows drew together in an outward sign of confusion. "Surgery?" she echoed. Why had she needed surgery? Her mind was a complete blank.

"That woman sank her pruning shears into your back up to the hilt." And then his silent promise to remain calm went up in smoke as the horror of losing her replayed itself in his head. "What the hell were you thinking of, diving in front of her like that?"

It suddenly came back to her. All of it. "I wasn't diving in front of her," she protested weakly. "I was pushing you out of the way." She paused to draw in a breath and winced as she did so. Every single breath hurt. "By the way, you're welcome," she said.

He couldn't bring himself to thank her for what she'd done because if she'd died, he would have never forgiven himself. And never felt whole again. "You could have been killed," he said angrily.

"So could you," she countered weakly. Another exhausted sigh escaped her lips. "If you're here to give me a hard time, could I have a rain check? I'm really not up to it."

That meant she couldn't argue back. "Couldn't think of a better time, then," he answered. And then his mouth softened into a smile. Moving his chair in closer, Tom lightly stroked her cheek with the back of his hand, thinking how lucky he was that he could do so. That she was still alive. "It was a stupid thing to do."

"Seemed smart on my end," she told him with effort. She couldn't remember it ever being this hard, this exhausting, to talk. "Couldn't let Tom Cavanaugh get killed on my watch. Your whole family would have come after me." The entire scene began to play itself over again in her head. Her eyes widened slightly as she remembered. Kait reached for his hand, clutching it. "Megan?"

He knew she was asking after the child's whereabouts. One of Andrew's daughters—Callie, he thought her name was—had taken the little girl to her house. "She's fine. You're her new hero."

Details flooded her brain. She had so much to do. "I have to call her parents, let them know we found her—"

She tried to get up again, but Tom gently pushed her back down.

"Already taken care of," he assured her. "I called her parents right after you came out of surgery." He couldn't think coherently before he knew that she'd pull through. "Megan's father arrived home from the Middle East just this morning. They're both taking the first flight out of New Mexico they can get. Bridget's on standby to pick them up the second they land."

Kait nodded and tried to smile. "That's good." The stabbing came back to her. "What about that woman?"

"You mean Greta?" he asked just to be clear what she was asking.

Kait set her mouth grimly. She would remember that awful guttural sound for a very long time. "Yeah, her."

He didn't want to talk about Greta right now and merely said, "She won't be bothering anyone anymore."

But Kait needed to know. "She's dead?"

He nodded grimly and was surprised to hear Kait murmur, "Poor woman."

"Why would you say that?" he asked. "She almost killed you."

That was only a piece of the story. There was more to it, the portion that tugged at her heart.

"She lost her daughter and grief pushed her over the edge." But there was one thing she couldn't understand. Megan had been a little girl living in a different state. Why had Greta specifically come after her? "But why did she take Megan? Why not some other little girl?"

He'd gotten the story from Brian, who'd had one of the other detectives interrogate Max Crammer. He was a broken man now that his wife was gone.

"Greta was visiting a relative in New Mexico when she saw Megan playing in the park with some friends. According to Max, Megan looked identical to the little girl she'd lost ten years ago. Greta followed her home to see where she lived, then called her husband. She told him that she'd found Sally and insisted that he drive out here 'in their white van.'"

"Why was she so specific?" Kait asked.

"Because that was the vehicle she was driving when she had the accident that killed her daughter. It wasn't some guy who hit her daughter with a car, *she* did. Crammer said that his wife had been sinking deeper and deeper into depression since their daughter's death and he was afraid for his wife's sanity. His wife was all he had and he was desperate to save her. He was afraid if he didn't find a way to keep her from sinking into a really black depression, she'd kill herself and he'd be all alone. That was why he did as she asked. He must have known she wanted to abduct the little girl," he guessed. "That was why he doctored the driver's license. Turns out he's some kind of a shady computer wizard, so it was pretty easy for him to falsify documents."

There was desperation and there was decency. From what she'd seen, Crammer didn't strike her as a cold-blooded kidnapper. "And he helped her kidnap Megan?" she asked incredulously.

Tom spread his hands. "It was either that or watch her go crazy."

There was no "go" about it, Kait thought. "She was already there."

Tom laughed shortly. "Yeah, but a lot of people live in the state of denial," he told her. "Especially when it comes to a loved one. But once his wife was dead, there was no reason for Crammer to lie to anyone anymore."

Finished with his explanation, Tom suddenly felt overwhelmed. He took her hand in his. God but she felt fragile, he couldn't help thinking. As fragile as life could sometimes be. He shook his head, thinking how close he'd come to losing her.

"I can't believe you actually did that."

She raised her eyes to his. He'd lost her. "Which part?"

There was only one part that mattered as far as he was concerned. "The part where you're throwing yourself between that knife and me."

"You threw yourself on top of me that first day—when that carjacker was going to shoot me, remember?" she reminded him pointedly. "I was just trying to return the favor."

So that was what she'd meant when she said they were even. He thought she was in shock. The woman was far too cavalier.

He reined in his anger because he knew that it was driven by fear. Fear that he could have lost her permanently. "That was different."

Her mouth felt dry but she forced the words out. "Why? Because you're a man?"

Frustrated, he said, "Shoot me, but yeah, because I'm a man and I'm supposed to be the protector."

She would have laughed if she could have, but she instinctively knew it would hurt too much. "And I'm a cop. I'm supposed to serve and protect."

He wouldn't accept that excuse from her. Her scream when the other woman drove the shears into her back was going to haunt him for a long, long time. "That applies to private citizens."

Weak, tired, she still refused to let him win the argument. "That applies to everybody," Kait contradicted. "News flash, Cavanaugh. It's the twenty-first century. We're equals. Some of us are just built a little softer than others."

Tom shook his head. "I'm never going to win an argument with you, am I?"

Maybe it was her weakened state, but that almost sounded as if he was talking about the future. A life together would be impossible. The case was over. And she was going home.

Still, she looked at him. "You make it sound as if arguing is going to be an ongoing thing between us."

He laughed shortly. "I figure, given your temperament, it will be."

He was just confusing her more. "You're planning on calling New Mexico to harass me?"

He answered her question with a question of his own. "You're planning on going back?"

Nothing was making sense to her right now. Her head was pounding. "Shouldn't I be?"

He didn't want to corner her, not in this condition because then she could always say that he took advantage of her in a weakened state. When she made her decision, he wanted her to be able to think clearly.

So all he said in response was, "I thought maybe you'd stick around here for a while."

"Why would I do that?" she asked him. "My job's back in New Mexico."

He noticed she didn't say that her life was back in New Mexico. At least that was a hopeful sign. "What if there was a job for you here?"

"Somebody need another knife blocked?" she asked wryly.

"No, but we could always use another good detective on the force," Brian said, answering her quip as he walked into her room. He smiled warmly at her. "How are you doing, Kaitlyn?"

She wanted to say "fine" but they all knew that was a lie. "It only hurts when I laugh."

"Then we'll try not to make you laugh," Brian promised.

Kait looked from the chief of detectives to his

nephew. Was it just her, or had they said what she thought they'd said? "Are you serious?"

"About not making you laugh?" Brian asked.

"No, the other thing." Maybe her mind *was* playing tricks on her. "About there being a job here."

"Just say the word," Brian told her. And then he added with knowing smile, "Oh, and by the way, I had a long talk with your lieutenant that first day you came here."

Groggy though she was, Kait knew that could only mean one thing. The lieutenant had told Brian that she was out here on vacation, not on official police business. "You knew."

Brian nodded. "I knew."

She didn't understand. "Then why—"

Brian kept his answer deliberately vague. "Sometimes a person has to do what they have to do. There was a child involved. I didn't think that a little slack was out of order."

She knew she'd liked the man for a reason. "Can we talk about the job later?" she asked. "I'm feeling a little tired right now."

"No problem," Brian said.

Or maybe it was Tom whom she heard. Kait couldn't be completely sure. Everything seemed rather fuzzy all of a sudden.

She drifted off the next moment.

Chapter 16

Kait felt something small and delicate brush against her face, like the fleeting kiss of a butterfly seeking some place to land. It slowly drew her out of the hazy, gauze-wrapped, shapeless universe she'd been time-lessly floating through.

With a start, Kait realized that she must have fallen asleep again. The last thing she could remember was seeing the chief of detectives and Tom in her room. Something about a job opening.

Or maybe she'd dreamed that because it had made her feel wanted.

But she wasn't dreaming the soft, fluttery movement along her cheek. She could *feel* it.

Her eyes were still closed. With effort, Kait opened them.

Megan was peering into her face. The moment she

opened her eyes, she saw the little girl smiling broadly at her.

"You opened your eyes. You're alive," Megan declared happily.

"I'm alive," Kait confirmed, the words inching their way up an oddly hoarse throat.

Still caught somewhere between dreams and reality, Kait blinked twice, trying to focus not just her eyes but her mind, as well. Both were still rather fuzzy.

As her vision cleared, she saw that beside Megan, the little girl's parents were standing around her bed. And Tom was in the background, standing off to the side. Watching her.

Kait tried to smile at Amanda and Derek, but she wasn't sure if the action was actually completed. She realized that Derek was still in his uniform. They must have come here directly from the airport.

What were they all doing here? Was she dying? She felt incredibly achy and confused. Was that how you felt when you were dying?

Amanda took her hand. "I don't know how to thank you, Kait," she said, tears filling her eyes. "I knew that when you made me that promise that you'd find our little girl. That you'd find Megan." Her voice hitched a little and it took her a second to continue. "You've never broken a promise to me—ever—but I'd be lying if I didn't tell you I was scared that maybe this time…." Amanda's voice trailed off. She couldn't finish her sentence.

Kait lightly squeezed the other woman's hand. It was all she had the strength for. "It's okay. I was scared, too," she admitted.

Amanda blinked back tears. "I guess Uncle Ron

knew what he was doing when he gave you my mom's name. It was like she was watching over both of us that way."

With effort, Kait nodded. "Yes, she was. Are you going to go back home now?" she asked. After all, there was nothing to keep them here now that they had been reunited with their daughter.

"Not right away," Derek told her. Reaching for her other hand, the corporal ever so slightly squeezed it in mute gratitude. Kait understood. "The corps's given me two weeks off to be with Mandy and Meggie, now that she's been found. And that chief of detectives that met us at the airport, he said we were welcome to spend Christmas with him and his family. He said that was where you'd be once they released you from here, so there's no way we could refuse."

Kait looked to Tom for an answer. Had she missed something? When had all this been decided? "I'm spending Christmas with your family?"

Tom could see what she was thinking. The case was solved, time for her to return to where she came from. Well, not if he could help it.

"Hey, you're in no condition to fly," he protested. "We had to pull strings to get you released to Brian."

"Honey, why don't we let cousin Kait rest?" Amanda suggested to her husband. "We can come by and see her later today." As she herded her daughter and her husband out, Amanda turned her head and mouthed, "Thank you from the bottom of my heart," to Kait.

Tom waited until the threesome had left the room and closed the door behind them. Only then did he come forward and sit down on the chair beside Kait's bed. He looked at her for a long moment.

"Cousin Kait, huh?" He already knew all about the connection. Brian had told him when he brought the family to the hospital, as he'd requested. When he'd initially made the suggestion, he'd thought it might help Kait to see the family being reunited in person. Now it was obviously more than just that. "You could have told me you were related to the victim."

"I didn't think you needed to know that," she said vaguely. And it would have meant sharing more of herself than she'd wanted to in the beginning. As they became closer, the revelation had felt awkward, so she'd just let it go.

"You don't get it yet, do you?" he asked her impatiently. "I *need* to know everything."

"But why?" she asked. What he said to her made no sense. "The case is over. We found Megan, remember?"

"The *case* is over," he echoed, putting emphasis where it belonged. "*We're* not over."

She searched his face, trying to grasp what he was saying. Afraid of getting it wrong. "What's that supposed to mean?"

Tom blew out a breath, silently cautioning himself to move slower. He had one shot at making his case and he didn't want to blow it. "What do you think it means?"

Oh, no, she wasn't going to get sucked into some kind of psychological babble. "I asked you first. Don't play games with me, Cavanaugh. I took a pruning shear for you." That had sounded way better in her head than it did on her tongue, she thought.

Humoring Kait, he spelled it out for her. "It means that my new uncle offered you a job on our police force. It means I want to know everything about *you,*" he said pointedly, then underscored it again. *"Everything."*

"Everything?"

"Everything," he repeated emphatically.

A half smile curved her dry lips. "You mean like that my real name was Bob?"

Tom could only stare at her, stunned. "Bob?" he echoed in confused disbelief.

"Bob," she affirmed. It was about the only time she ever remembered her grandmother explaining anything to her. "My grandmother named me after her boyfriend. When he rescued me from them, Ronald made sure that he changed my name for me. He named me after his late sister." Her smile deepened as she remembered the man who had been so kind to her when he could have just walked away. "Years later, he told me that she'd died from a brain tumor a few months before he rescued me. He said if he was ever going to have a daughter, he would want to name her after his sister."

Tom was still trying to understand why anyone in their right mind would name a little girl Bob. "Your name was actually *Bob?*"

She'd made a mistake, exposed too much. "Okay, maybe that was too much information," she said, upbraiding herself.

"There's no such thing," Tom told her, his tone deadly serious. "And I meant what I said. I want to know *everything* about you, no matter how insignificant or trivial you might think it is."

Was he conducting some kind of an investigation on her? Her head was beginning to ache. "Why?"

He looked straight into her eyes. "Why do you think?"

She blew out a breath, tired. "Why are you always

answering questions with questions? Just tell me what you mean."

"Okay," he replied gamely. *Here goes nothing.* "I mean to convince you to stay here in Aurora. I mean to be part of every day of the rest of your life until one of us is dead. Is that clear enough for you?"

"Actually, no." She paused for half a second, running her tongue along her dry lips. "Are you recruiting me for the police force or asking me to marry you?"

"Both," he said simply. "But mainly the latter—when you're ready," he added quickly. "I don't want to rush you. We'll take it one day at a time and you'll see how you feel about it down the road." Waiting was going to kill him, but he didn't want her to feel as if he was pressuring her to say yes. It wouldn't count then. When she said yes to him, as he felt in his heart she eventually would, he wanted her to be healed, not vulnerable. He didn't want her thinking someday that he'd taken advantage of the situation and rushed her into marrying him when she wasn't thinking clearly.

She wasn't imagining it. He was asking her to marry him. Her heart began to beat harder as she absorbed the idea. But she couldn't just jump at the chance. If she seemed too willing, it would give him the upper hand and put her at a disadvantage. A lifetime of training was hard to turn her back on.

"So, just so I'm clear, this is your idea of a proposal?"

"This is my way of giving you fair warning that I mean to ask you to marry me sometime in the not-too-distant future. To ask you now, in this hospital room, while you're still groggy from the surgery, wouldn't seem right." He took her hand in his. "I like what we have here and I'd like to see where it goes. I can't do that if you go back to New Mexico."

"Is that why you had your uncle offer me a job?" she wanted to know.

Tom laughed at the very thought. "Brian Cavanaugh is a kind man and a great chief of detectives, but *no one* ever makes him do what he doesn't want to do. No, the job offer came from him. You impressed him."

"How?" she asked incredulously. "With the skillful way I blocked a pair of pruning shears?"

He didn't want her making light of what she'd done by tracking down the little girl—even if she was her niece. "With your police work, with your diligence and with your loyalty. You're not a nine-to-five cop, you're a twenty-four/seven law-enforcement officer. That means something to the chief," he told her with feeling. "There's a reason why the Aurora Police Department is ranked one of the finest in the country. The chief likes stocking it with the best of the best." And that was clearly her. "So, what's your answer?"

She looked at him for a long moment. Was he referring to the veiled marriage proposal, or just the job offer? "What was the question again?"

He smiled at her. She was trying to get him to back off. "For now, it's will you stay in Aurora?" he answered, his eyes never leaving hers.

Her pulse, she found, was still beating somewhat erratically. "And for later?"

"Will be for later," he replied after a beat.

Kait took a deep breath. "I guess I'll stay," she finally said. "Otherwise," she added significantly, "I won't find out about 'later.'"

Tom laughed. "I had no idea that you had this streak of overwhelming curiosity."

She smiled then, lighting up the room, as well as his world. "Neither did I until just now."

A wave of emotion swept over him when he thought of how very close he'd come to almost losing her. He wanted to hold her to him, to hold on to Kait tightly and not let go, but he knew she was still too fragile for that. Still, there was this desire, this craving within him that grew larger by the minute. Any second now, it would reach proportions that would be out of control.

To forestall that, he asked, "Would you mind very much if I kissed you now?"

Her eyes all but laughed at him. "I'd mind very much if you didn't," she answered in a soft, sultry whisper that punched him right in his solar plexus.

"Can't have that," he murmured just before he framed Kait's face and pressed his lips to hers.

He had no way of knowing that at that moment, her heart was rejoicing just as much as his.

Epilogue

"Are you tired?" Tom whispered the words against her ear, sending warm waves through her.

"My answer's still the same," Kait told him, referring to the fact that he'd already asked her that twice before and she'd said no each time.

After her release from the hospital, true to his word, Tom's uncle Brian had insisted that she remain with them until she had completely recovered.

Consequently, she found herself in the thick of things as Brian and his wife, Lila, aided and abetted by Andrew and Rose, hosted the Christmas Day festivities. Something, she quickly discovered, was actually a two-day affair running from Christmas Eve morning until Christmas Day night. There was endless food, endless conversation and endless Cavanaughs as well as anyone who wanted to drop by for a minute or a day.

"How about some air, then?" Tom asked, nodding toward the patio.

She sensed his tension and wondered what he was up to. "Some air would be nice," she allowed.

Since the operation was just a week behind her, Tom offered her his arm.

Taking it, she carefully rose to her feet. The last thing she wanted was to call attention to herself by being pitched facedown if her knees decided to buckle. She still wasn't as strong as she would have liked.

The moment they were outside, he gently guided her to a chair, then dragged over another so that he could sit beside her.

"What's on your mind?" she asked.

"What makes you think there's something on my mind?" he asked her.

She smiled, hoping he wasn't about to drop some bombshell on her she couldn't handle. "Because I don't think your objective was just securing cooler air."

He paused a moment, pulling himself together. He'd faced down gunmen with cooler nerves than what he was experiencing right now.

All the arguments he'd given himself a week ago still held—but he had discovered that he possessed an impatient streak. One that was giving him no peace until he finally asked her the all-important question he'd promised himself he wouldn't ask for at least a month.

The month had morphed into three weeks. And then two and now here he was at one. It was as long as he could hold out.

"I know I said I wouldn't ask for a while, but I can't help it." He looked at her intently. "I'm asking now. Will you?"

It took her a couple of seconds to put the pieces together. Boy, he really was bad at this, wasn't he? Keeping a straight face, she asked, "By any chance, are you asking me to marry you?"

"Yes," he answered guardedly. When he saw the amusement in her eyes, he protested, "Hey, I've never done this before. I'm winging it here."

Yes, he was, she thought. But just this once, she needed the words. Needed them to convince herself that this wasn't something, at bottom, that she was just conjuring up in her head. "You could try saying 'Will you marry me?' I've heard that generally works."

Did that mean she was ready to say yes? Because God knew *he* was ready.

"Okay." He took Kait's hand in his. "Will you marry me?"

It was a very bare sentence. She needed to hear more. Needed him to say things that she would always remember. "Why?" she prodded.

He stared at her. Had he misread the signals? "What do you mean, why?"

Kait took a deep breath and then said, "Why do you want me to marry you?"

What did she mean, why? Why did she think? For the oldest reason in the world. "Damn it, because I love you," he shouted. And then it all came pouring out. "Because when I heard you scream that day, I thought that crazy woman had killed you." That had been, hands down, the worst moment of his entire life. "And I didn't want to live anymore," he admitted quietly.

For a second, overcome, Kait said nothing. And then, taking a breath to steady herself, she said, "Okay, then. I guess my answer's yes."

That wasn't quite the response he was expecting. "You 'guess'?"

Kait struggled to keep just a little of her protective barrier around her. She hated being completely vulnerable. "Hey, don't push it, Cavanaugh. I'm new to this emotions stuff, remember? You're going to have to be content with baby steps."

He inclined his head, indicating that he was willing to go along with that, as long as he had some assurances. "Do any of these 'baby steps' eventually lead to you telling me you love me?"

Her eyes were smiling at him even though she was trying to look serious. "You play your cards right, and then yeah, they might."

He was still holding her hand. "Could I have a preview?"

"Only if you kiss me," she bargained.

"That could be arranged," he replied, his mouth inches from hers.

Her heart began tap-dancing in her chest. "Okay, I love you. You can be a real pain in the butt sometimes, and you keep wheedling things out of me that I have no intentions of saying and God knows I should have my head examined but, yes, I love you." Taking another breath, her eyes pinned him. "Satisfied?"

"Not yet, but I'll get there."

"And how do you propose to do that?" Kait asked.

Tom gave up the act and grinned broadly. "Hell, I thought you'd never ask."

And with that he drew even closer, dragging his chair up against hers. Their knees touched, and he framed her face in his hands and kissed her gently on the lips.

The sigh was trapped in her throat, but she did what she could to disguise it. "You can do better than that, Cavanaugh. I promise I won't break."

He smiled into her eyes. "And, as I recall, you're the lady who never breaks a promise," he whispered as he brought his lips down on hers.

This time, they both forgot all about being gentle.

* * * * *

SUSPENSE

Heartstopping stories of intrigue and mystery—
where true love always triumphs.

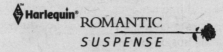

COMING NEXT MONTH
AVAILABLE DECEMBER 27, 2011

#1687 TOOL BELT DEFENDER
Lawmen of Black Rock
Carla Cassidy

#1688 SPECIAL AGENT'S PERFECT COVER
Perfect, Wyoming
Marie Ferrarella

#1689 SOLDIER'S RESCUE MISSION
H.O.T. Watch
Cindy Dees

#1690 THE HEARTBREAK SHERIFF
Small-Town Scandals
Elle Kennedy

HRSCNM1211

REQUEST YOUR FREE BOOKS!
2 FREE NOVELS PLUS 2 FREE GIFTS!

Harlequin®

ROMANTIC
SUSPENSE
Sparked by Danger, Fueled by Passion.

YES! Please send me 2 FREE Harlequin® Romantic Suspense novels and my 2 FREE gifts (gifts are worth about $10). After receiving them, if I don't wish to receive any more books, I can return the shipping statement marked "cancel." If I don't cancel, I will receive 4 brand-new novels every month and be billed just $4.49 per book in the U.S. or $5.24 per book in Canada. That's a saving of at least 14% off the cover price! It's quite a bargain! Shipping and handling is just 50¢ per book in the U.S. and 75¢ per book in Canada.* I understand that accepting the 2 free books and gifts places me under no obligation to buy anything. I can always return a shipment and cancel at any time. Even if I never buy another book, the two free books and gifts are mine to keep forever.

240/340 HDN FEFR

Name _____ (PLEASE PRINT)

Address _____ Apt. #

City _____ State/Prov. _____ Zip/Postal Code

Signature (if under 18, a parent or guardian must sign)

Mail to the **Reader Service:**
IN U.S.A.: P.O. Box 1867, Buffalo, NY 14240-1867
IN CANADA: P.O. Box 609, Fort Erie, Ontario L2A 5X3

Not valid for current subscribers to Harlequin Romantic Suspense books.

Want to try two free books from another line?
Call 1-800-873-8635 or visit www.ReaderService.com.

* Terms and prices subject to change without notice. Prices do not include applicable taxes. Sales tax applicable in N.Y. Canadian residents will be charged applicable taxes. Offer not valid in Quebec. This offer is limited to one order per household. All orders subject to credit approval. Credit or debit balances in a customer's account(s) may be offset by any other outstanding balance owed by or to the customer. Please allow 4 to 6 weeks for delivery. Offer available while quantities last.

Your Privacy—The Reader Service is committed to protecting your privacy. Our Privacy Policy is available online at www.ReaderService.com or upon request from the Reader Service.

We make a portion of our mailing list available to reputable third parties that offer products we believe may interest you. If you prefer that we not exchange your name with third parties, or if you wish to clarify or modify your communication preferences, please visit us at www.ReaderService.com/consumerschoice or write to us at Reader Service Preference Service, P.O. Box 9062, Buffalo, NY 14269. Include your complete name and address.

HRS11B

Harlequin®

INTRIGUE

USA TODAY BESTSELLING AUTHOR

DELORES FOSSEN

CONTINUES HER THRILLING MINISERIES

THE LAWMEN OF SILVER CREEK *Ranch*

When the unthinkable happens and children are stolen
from a local day care, old rivals Lieutenant Nate Ryland
and Darcy Burkhart team up to find their kids.
Danger lurks at every turn, but will Nate and Darcy
be able to catch the kidnappers before
the kidnappers catch them?

NATE

Find out this January!

*Brittany Grayson survived a horrible ordeal at the hands
of a serial killer known as The Professional…
who's after her now?*

*Harlequin® Romantic Suspense presents a new installment
in Carla Cassidy's reader-favorite miniseries,*
LAWMEN OF BLACK ROCK.

Enjoy a sneak peek of
TOOL BELT DEFENDER.

*Available January 2012
from Harlequin® Romantic Suspense.*

"**B**rittany?" His voice was deep and pleasant and made
her realize she'd been staring at him openmouthed through
the screen door.

"Yes, I'm Brittany and you must be…" Her mind suddenly went blank.

"Alex. Alex Crawford, Chad's friend. You called him
about a deck?"

As she unlocked the screen, she realized she wasn't
quite ready yet to allow a stranger inside, especially a male
stranger.

"Yes, I did. It's nice to meet you, Alex. Let's walk around
back and I'll show you what I have in mind," she said. She
frowned as she realized there was no car in her driveway.
"Did you walk here?" she asked.

His eyes were a warm blue that stood out against his
tanned face and was complemented by his slightly shaggy
dark hair. "I live three doors up." He pointed up the street to
the Walker home that had been on the market for a while.

"How long have you lived there?"

"I moved in about six weeks ago," he replied as they

walked around the side of the house.

That explained why she didn't know the Walkers had moved out and Mr. Hard Body had moved in. Six weeks ago she'd still been living at her brother Benjamin's house trying to heal from the trauma she'd lived through.

As they reached the backyard she motioned toward the broken brick patio just outside the back door. "What I'd like is a wooden deck big enough to hold a barbecue pit and an umbrella table and, of course, lots of people."

He nodded and pulled a tape measure from his tool belt. "An outdoor entertainment area," he said.

"Exactly," she replied and watched as he began to walk the site. The last thing Brittany had wanted to think about over the past eight months of her life was men. But looking at Alex Crawford definitely gave her a slight flutter of pure feminine pleasure.

Will Brittany be able to heal in the arms of Alex, her hotter-than-sin handyman...or will a second psychopath silence her forever? Find out in
TOOL BELT DEFENDER
Available January 2012
from Harlequin® Romantic Suspense
wherever books are sold.

HRSEXP0112

SPECIAL EDITION

Life, Love and Family

Karen Templeton

introduces

The FORTUNES *of* TEXAS: Whirlwind Romance

When a tornado destroys Red Rock, Texas,
Christina Hastings finds herself trapped in the
rubble with telecommunications heir
Scott Fortune. He's handsome, smart and
everything Christina has learned to guard herself
against. As they await rescue, an unlikely attraction
forms between the two and Scott soon finds
himself wanting to know about this mysterious
beauty. But can he catch Christina before she runs
away from her true feelings?

FORTUNE'S CINDERELLA

Available December 27th wherever books are sold!

SSE65643